BEAUTIFUL

AMY REED

SIMON PULSE
NEW YORK LONDON TORONTO SYDNEY

SIMON PULSE

An imprint of Simon & Schuster Children's Publishing Division
1230 Avenue of the Americas, New York, NY 10020
First Simon Pulse hardcover edition October 2009
Copyright © 2009 by Amy Reed
SIMON PULSE and colophon are registered trademarks
of Simon & Schuster, Inc.
For information about special discounts for bulk purchases, please contact Simon &
Schuster Special Sales at 1-866-506-1949 or business@simonandschuster.com.
The Simon & Schuster Speakers Bureau can bring authors to your live event. For
more information or to book an event contact the Simon & Schuster Speakers
Bureau at 1-866-248-3049 or visit our website at www.simonspeakers.com.
Designed by Mike Rosamilia
The text of this book was set in Adobe Garamond Pro.
Manufactured in the United States of America
6 8 10 9 7 5
Library of Congress Cataloging-in-Publication Data
Reed, Amy.
Beautiful / Amy Reed.
p. cm.
Summary: Haunted by serious problems in her recent past,
thirteen-year-old Cassie makes a fresh start at a Seattle school but is drawn by
dangerous new friends into a world of sex, drugs, and violence, while her parents
remain oblivious.
[1. Emotional problems—Fiction. 2. Sex—Fiction.
3. Drug abuse—Fiction. 4. Self-esteem—Fiction.
5. Family problems—Fiction. 6. Seattle (Wash.)—Fiction.] I. Title.
PZ7.R2462Bec 2009
[Fic]—dc22
2008040680
ISBN 978-1-4169-7830-5
ISBN 978-1-4169-8530-3 (eBook)

This book is dedicated to the girls—beautiful, all of us

(ONE)

I don't see her coming.

I am looking at my piece of pizza. I am watching pepperoni glisten. It is my third day at the new school and I am sitting at a table next to the bathrooms. I am eating lunch with the blond girls with the pink sweaters, the girls who talk incessantly about Harvard even though we're only in seventh grade. They are the kind of girls who have always ignored me. But these girls are different than the ones on the island. They think I am one of them.

She grabs my shoulder from behind and I jump. I turn around. She says, "What's your name?"

I tell her, "Cassie."

She says, "Alex."

She is wearing an army jacket, a short jean skirt, fishnet stockings, and combat boots. Her hair is shoulder length, frizzy and green. She's tall and skinny, not skinny like a model but skinny like a boy. Her blue eyes are so pale they don't look human and her eyelashes and eyebrows are so blond they're almost white. She is not pretty, not even close to pretty. But there's something about her that's bigger than pretty, something bigger than smart girls going to Harvard.

It's only my third day, but I knew the second I got here that this place was different. It is not like the island, not a place ruled by good girls. I saw Alex. I saw the ninth grade boys she hangs out with, their multicolored hair, their postures of indifference, their clothes that tell everybody they're too cool to care. I heard her loud voice drowning everything out. I saw how other girls let her cut in front of them in line. I saw everyone else looking at her, looking at the boys with their lazy confidence, everyone looking and trying not to be seen.

I saw them at the best table in the cafeteria and I decided to change. It is not hard to change when you were never anything in the first place. It is not hard to put on a T-shirt of a band you overheard the cool kids talking about, to wear tight jeans with holes, to walk by their table and make sure they see you. All it takes is moving off an island to a suburb of Seattle where no one knows who you were before.

"You're in seventh grade." She says this as a statement.

"Yes," I answer.

The pink-sweater girls are looking at me like they made a big mistake.

"Where are you from?" she says.

"Bainbridge Island."

"I can tell," she says. "Come with me." She grabs my wrist and my plastic fork drops. "I have some people who want to meet you."

I'm supposed to stand up now. I'm supposed to leave the pizza and the smart girls and go with the girl named Alex to the people who want to meet me. I cannot look back, not at the plate of greasy pizza and the girls who were almost my friends. Just follow Alex. Keep walking. One step. Two steps. I must focus on my face not turning red. Focus on breathing. Stand up straight. Remember, this is what you want.

The boys are getting bigger. I must pretend I don't notice their stares. I cannot turn red. I cannot smile the way I do when I'm nervous, with my cheeks twitching, my lips curled all awkward and lopsided. I must ignore the burn where Alex holds my wrist too tight. I cannot wonder why she's holding my wrist the way she does, why she doesn't trust me to walk on my own, why she keeps looking back at me, why she won't let me out of her sight. I cannot think of maybes. I cannot think of "What if I turned around right now? What if I went the other way?" There is no other way. There is only forward, with Alex, to the boys who want to meet me.

I am slowing down. I have stopped. I am looking at big sneakers on ninth grade boys. Legs attached. Other things. Chests, arms, faces. Eyes looking. Droopy, red, big-boy eyes. Smiles. Hands on my shoulders. Pushing, guiding, driving me.

"James, this is Cassie, the beautiful seventh grader," Alex says. Hair shaved on the side, mohawk in the middle, face pretty and flawless. This one's the cutest. This one's the leader.

"Wes, this is Cassie, the beautiful seventh grader." Pants baggy, legs spread, lounging with arms open, baby-fat face. Not a baby, dangerous. He smiles. They all smile.

Jackson, Anthony. I remember their names. They say, "Sit down." I do what they say. Alex nods her approval.

I must not look up from my shoes. I must pretend I don't feel James's leg touching mine, his mouth so close to my ear. Don't see Alex whispering to him. Don't feel the stares. Don't hear the laughing. Just remember what Mom says about my "almond eyes," my "dancer's body," my "high cheekbones," my "long neck," my hair, my lips, my breasts, all of the things I have now that I didn't have before.

"Cassie," James says, and my name sounds like flowers in his mouth.

"Yes." I look at his chiseled chin. I look at his teeth, perfect and white. I do not look at his eyes.

"Are you straight?" he says, and I compute in my head what this question might mean, and I say, "Yes, well, I think so," because I think he wants to know if I like boys. I look at his eyes and know I have made a mistake. They are green and smiling and curious, wanting me to answer correctly. He says, "I mean, are you a good girl? Or do you do bad things?"

"What do you mean by bad things?" is what I want to say, but I don't say anything. I just look at him, hoping he cannot read my mind, cannot smell my terror, will not now realize that I do not deserve this attention, that he's made a mistake by looking at me in this not-cruel way.

"I mean, I noticed you the last couple of days. You seemed like a good girl. But today you look different."

It is true. I am different from what I was yesterday and all the days before that.

"So, are you straight?" he says. "I mean, do you do drugs and stuff?"

"Yeah, um, I guess so." I haven't. I will. Yes. I will do anything he wants. I will sit here while everyone stares at me. I will sit here until the bell rings and it is time to go back to class and the girl named Alex says, "Give me your number," and I do.

. . .

Even though no one else talks to me for the rest of the day, I hold on to "beautiful." I hold on to lunch tomorrow at the best table in the cafeteria. Even though I ride the bus home alone and watch the marina and big houses go by, there are ninth grade boys somewhere who may be thinking about me.

Even though Mom's asleep and Dad's at work, even though there are still boxes piled everywhere from the move, even though Mom's too sad to cook and I eat peanut butter for dinner, and Dad doesn't come home until the house is dark, and the walls are too thin to keep out the yelling, even though I can hear my mom crying, there is a girl somewhere who has my number. There are ninth grade boys who will want it. There are ninth grade boys who may be thinking about me, making me exist somewhere other than here, making me something bigger than the flesh in the corner of this room. There is a picture of me in their heads, a picture of someone I don't know yet. She is not the chubby girl with the braces and bad perm. She is not the girl hiding in the bathroom at recess. She is someone new, a blank slate they have named beautiful. That is what I am now: beautiful, with this new body and face and hair and clothes. Beautiful, with this erasing of history.

(TWO)

When we get to my

house, I take Alex straight to my room. I don't show her Mom asleep on the couch or the boxes piled around the apartment or the orange carpet in my parents' room or their one small window that lets in no light, the bathroom with peeling linoleum, the kitchen that smells like mildew, the deck that barely fits our barbecue and a couple of plastic chairs. I just take her to my room that I went to work on as soon as we got here, the room I could not sleep in until everything was put away, until the posters were all put up straight, the books alphabetized on the bookshelves and sectioned into subject matter and country of origin, the bed made, the clothes folded and tucked into drawers, and everything exactly the way it should be. That was two weeks ago, but there are still boxes everywhere and Mom's still putting the living room together even though she has nothing to do all day except watch TV and play video games.

Alex hasn't said anything about the posters on my wall, the ones of cool bands I've never even listened to but made Mom buy me at the mall. She doesn't notice the incense burner or candles or the magazine cutouts of rock stars who look like drug addicts. All she does is laugh and say, "You still have stuffed animals?" and I laugh and say, "I've been meaning to get rid of them," and I shove them in the garbage can even though they don't fit and I have to keep pushing them in while Alex walks around and touches everything. She pulls books out of my bookshelf and does not put them back in alphabetical order.

"This one's fucking thick," she says.

"It's one of my favorite books," I tell her. "It's about the French Revolution when all the poor people rebelled against the government and this guy who used to be a criminal escaped from prison and became good and—"

"You are such a nerd," she says with a look on her face like she is starting to think she made a mistake about me. She turns around and keeps looking through my shelves until she finds my photo album and says, "Ooh, what's this?" and I tell her nothing because there is nothing I can say except lies. She takes it out and sits down and stops talking to me. I sit on my bed, not breathing, waiting for the discovery, waiting for the serious look on her face to change and turn into laughter.

I can hear my mom shuffling around in the living room. Something crashes and I hear her say "Shit." Alex laughs but she does not look up.

"Why are you in those classes?" she says as she continues to flip through the photo album of the girls who were never my friends.

"What classes?"

"The ones for smart kids." She pulls out a picture of Angela from back home, the most popular girl in school. Angela's wearing a cashmere sweater and skirt. Her hair is blond and perfect and she has a look on her face like anything is possible. I am suddenly embarrassed for her, embarrassed for her confidence and the sun shining on her hair, embarrassed for her soft pink skin. She has no idea there's a place like here, a place where she is nothing. There are a lot of photos of her in my album, taken at the sixth-grade picnic, at the school play when she was the star, at elementary school graduation. There are no pictures of me. I am always behind the camera. I am always somewhere no one can see me.

Alex tears the picture in half, then in half again. I think it must be a joke, that it was only a piece of paper she tore. The picture must be somewhere still whole.

"Why'd you do that?" I ask her.

"I don't like her," she answers, and I look in her hands, and Angela is torn into four jagged pieces. "Tell me why you're in the smart classes," she says.

"I don't know."

"Are you smart?" she says, like she's asking if I'm retarded.

"No. Yes. I don't know." She is tearing the picture into even smaller pieces. She is looking at me while she does this, tearing slowly and smiling.

"Did your parents make you take those classes?"

"Yes," I say, even though it's not really true, and the answer seems to satisfy her.

"I wish we had classes together," she says, holding up another picture.

"Me too," I say. I cannot look upset about the picture. I must act like I know it is funny. I must act like I care about nothing.

"Who's this?" she says.

"That's Leslie," I tell her, and for some reason I add, "She's my best friend." She wasn't as popular as Angela, but she was always my favorite. She was the nicest one in the group, not as rich as the others and kind of quiet. "We're at the sixth grade picnic and we're at the beach on the weekend before the end of school and Derrick Jenson just kicked the ball into the water and—"

"Let's burn her," Alex says.

"What?" She is crumpling up Leslie in her hand.

"Let's burn all of them. They're not your friends anymore, are they?"

"Why not?"

"You live here now."

"We can still be friends."

"No you can't. They're on *Bainbridge.*" She says the name of the island like I should be ashamed of it, like it's beneath her, like anything from there is not welcome here. And even though it's only on the other side of Seattle, I know that I will never go back. There is nothing there for me, nothing for my mother or father. There is a lake and land and salt water between us. There is a bridge and a ferryboat and trees and dirt roads. There is a whole other world with an entirely different version of me, a me that is not pretty, a me that no boys want, a me she would never talk to. The truth is far worse than she thinks. I am something worse than a preppy girl from an island. I am an ugly girl from an island. I am a girl who can't talk. I am a girl with a photo album full of people who don't even know who I am.

I don't want Alex seeing any more of the pictures. She is right. They are not real. They are not my life. This is my life now and it is better than the pretend one. Alex is better than Leslie and Angela and all the other girls who never existed as anything except snapshots taken in secret, backs walking away, distant echoes of giggles. They are gone. They do not exist. They never existed.

"I'm your friend now, right?" she says.

"Yes."

"So you don't need them."

"No."

Alex tells me to tell my mom we're going for a walk. She puts the photo album in her backpack. Mom is putting framed pictures on top of the fake fireplace, the same ones that used to be on top of our old, real fireplace. There is a picture of her holding me as a baby when she was skinny and beautiful. There's one of my dad when he still had a beard, sitting in a big chair I don't recognize. There's one of all of us standing by the Christmas tree, my mom's hands on my shoulders with a big smile like she's the happiest she's ever been, like she doesn't even notice that I look scared and my dad looks angry like he always does.

We walk up the hill to the train tracks behind my apartment building. We can see Lake Washington and the whole city from up here, but it looks different from when I saw it from the island. All of the buildings are backward.

We sit down on the train tracks and Alex hands me a lighter and says, "Burn them." She starts tearing the pictures out of the album and handing them to me, one by one. I hold them in my hand, the girls I watched for years, the girls I dreamt of being, the good girls, the girls who will never know me. They are over water, through trees. They are not my friends. She is. Alex is. She is my only friend.

I am surprised how easily they burn, how quickly their faces turn to gray ash in my hands. When we are done, there is a pile of charred remains by my feet. They are ghosts of people I never knew, which the rain will wash away.

Alex throws the empty album into the bushes. The sun is starting to set and the bridge twinkles with commuters from Seattle. One of them could be my dad. But he's probably still at the office. I will probably not see him tonight.

"What time's your curfew?" Alex asks as she stands up.

"I don't really have one." I don't tell her it's because I've never needed one. I don't tell her it's because I've never had anywhere to go.

"Do you have any money?" she says.

"Eight dollars."

"That's good enough."

We walk down the hill and along the waterfront where Canada geese are squawking and crapping on the grass. We walk past the burger place, where we can see families eating through the windows. "Look at those assholes," Alex says.

I say, "Yeah."

There's a store that sells supplies to make your own wine. There's a restaurant with a menu in the window, where the salads cost fifteen dollars. We walk past these places to the corner with the 7-Eleven and the video arcade. There are no families here. This is where the town ends. There are little boys inside the arcade. There are big boys outside.

"Most of them are high schoolers," Alex tells me. They are smoking and drinking out of paper bags.

I have never done anything interesting in my life, but I am going to. I am going to be one of them. I am going to do things.

There's a fat guy sitting in the middle of the sidewalk with a rat crawling across his shoulders and down his back, over his lap and up his chest. It settles on top of his head and looks at us with the same beady eyes as the boy. The rat is purple like the fat boy's hair. It settles in like camouflage.

"Purple Haze," says Alex.

"What do you want?" he says. His voice is high and nasal. His face is greasy and pockmarked.

"Four hits," she says, and I have no idea what she's talking about.

"Heard anything from your brother?" the fat boy says.

"He's in Portland."

"I know that," he says, rolling his eyes.

"He's got a good job."

"No he doesn't."

"Yes he does."

"He's a junkie who lives in a warehouse and beats up fat people for fun," the fat boy says, like it's the funniest thing he ever heard.

"No he doesn't."

"He's in a gang against fat people."

"Where'd you hear that?"

"Classified information."

"Give me a cigarette," Alex says.

"Only if your friend will kiss me."

She looks at me. I shake my head.

"Just give me a cigarette."

He pulls one out and hands it to me. "My dear," he says, and offers to light it. I put it in my mouth and suck like I've seen my mom do.

"Can we have the acid now?" says Alex.

"Do you have money?"

"She does."

He looks me up and down and the fat under his chin wiggles like Jell-O. "I'll give it to you for free if you two make out," he says, and the smoke from the cigarette goes too far into my lungs and I start coughing.

"I'm not a dyke, fucker," says Alex.

"She's not inhaling," says Purple Haze, and points at me.

"What?"

"Your pretty friend. She doesn't know how to smoke."

Alex looks at me like I've done something terrible. I hand her the cigarette, and my face burns.

"Look, she's blushing," says Purple Haze. "Isn't that cute."

"Just give us the acid," Alex says, exhaling smoke like she knows what she's doing. Everyone is watching. I know they're thinking about what a fool I am. They're thinking I don't belong here. They're thinking, *Go back where you came from, little girl.*

"Have you ever taken a shit that was so good it was better than an orgasm?" says Purple Haze. "Like those really fat long ones that last forever and it feels like you lost like ten pounds?"

"Give him the money," Alex says to me. I open my purse and take out my wallet. My hands are shaking.

"Easy, girl. Sit here next to me."

I look at Alex. She nods.

I sit down even though my skirt is short. I put my purse in my lap to hide the place that is not covered. Purple Haze leans over and whispers in my ear, "Take it out slowly and reach over and put it in my pocket." I do what he says. His jeans are too warm and slightly moist. He smells like salami.

From his other pocket, he pulls out a makeup compact. He takes out two tiny cellophane packets with his fat fingers and puts them in my hand. "Have a nice trip, ladies." I stand up and dust off my skirt. I am trying not to shake. They're thinking, *Go home, little girl.* I don't look at Alex or Purple Haze as I start walking. I don't look at any of the high school boys even though their eyes burn holes into me. *Go home.*

"She doesn't talk much," I hear Purple Haze say behind me, even though I'm already halfway down the block.

"Wait!" yells Alex. I keep walking. I am still too close. If I stop walking, I will start crying and everyone will see me.

"What's your problem?" she says when she catches up to me.

"I just wanted to leave."

"You have to wait for me," she says.

"I'm sorry."

She stops walking and so do I. She is looking me in the eyes. She is looking at me like she hates me. "Don't do it again," she says. Her voice is hard, not like a girl's. I look at the ground and feel my body crumbling, turning into small, invisible pieces.

"Sorry," I say. I look up and expect her to be gone, but she is still there, smiling like nothing happened. I am solid again. She takes my hand and pulls it gently.

"Let's go in here," she says.

We slide between a closed boutique and a fancy cheese store. In the shadows Alex says, "Where's the acid?" I hold out my hand with the two little cellophane packets. "You take one and I'll take two." She opens a packet and licks it. The two tiny white paper squares stick to her tongue. She opens the second packet and presses her finger inside. One square sticks and she points it at me. "Here," she says.

"What?" I say.

"Eat it."

I lick her finger and it is salty.

"Am I supposed to swallow it?"

"Just let it dissolve."

"Where are we going now?"

"James's house."

I say "Shit," and it sounds ridiculous coming out of my mouth.

"You look good," Alex says. "Don't worry. He already wants you."

She walks fast and I try to keep up, but I am dizzy with "he wants you." It is good that she's so far ahead, that she can't see the stupid smile on my face.

"It's only about a mile," she says, and we don't talk until we get there.

We walk along the lake, on the sidewalk made for joggers and mothers with strollers. It's strange how different the shore is here, all perfect and straight. Instead of sharp rocks, instead of seaweed and barnacles and other live things, this beach is flat and sandy and barren, marked only with goose crap and the occasional piece of litter.

Here I am with the first friend I've had in forever. Here I am on my way to meet a boy who wants me. My life on the island is over. I have a new face and a new body and new clothes. I have a new friend and nothing will ever be the same again.

(THREE)

James's house is in a development full of mansions, down the hill from my apartment building, on the lake where the big houses stare at Seattle, brand-new with naked dirt yards no one's had time to plant anything in.

The shadows that cling to the side of the house start moving and I can't tell if I see James or darkness shaped like him. It feels like the ground is breathing and the air has hands, like everything is moving except me, like I am the only thing solid, like it is the rest of the world that is dizzy.

I say, "I feel weird."

Alex says, "It's working."

"Hi," James says, and he looks at me like he's a movie star.

Something is off about the way he leans against the house, like his hips are out of joint, like his body is overextended and struggling to stay upright. He's wearing a plain black sweatshirt, a baseball hat over his mohawk. He could be anyone right now. He could be normal, anonymous. I start laughing because suddenly he doesn't seem so tough. I laugh because suddenly everything's colored like a cartoon. I laugh because it's the only thing to do when your legs give up and you fall on the ground, when you're an idiot and you know you're an idiot and everyone around you is an idiot and there's nothing you can do about it.

I am on the ground. I am looking up at James's giant moon head and he is not laughing. He is looking at me like I have done something wrong, like I am not Cassie the Beautiful Seventh Grader, and all of a sudden none of this is funny and I want to cry.

"What did you do to her?" he says to Alex. He is angry. He is going to hurt us.

"What do you mean?" she says, and for some reason I hate her. I grab her hand anyway and she pulls it away, and I know I am supposed to stay on the ground.

"What the fuck did you do to her?" He is holding her by the shoulders. He is shaking her hard. Her head rolls around.

"Ow," she says, like she is starting to think about not laughing.

"You ruined her, you fucking bitch. You ruined her," is what he says, like it is the worst line from the worst movie ever made. I cannot hear what they say anymore because my ears are full of dirt. I can feel the ground and I wish it were mud so I could roll around in it, so I could be covered in brown. I could run away and be invisible in the dark. I could live in the trees and no one would find me. I am planning this. I am taking notes in my head to remember later. I don't know what I will eat, but I've heard there are people who eat worms, bugs, rodents. I will eat these things. I will need nothing.

I cannot hear but I can see Alex talking her way out of something. I can see James calming down like she's got a spell on him. I can see her giving him the other piece of acid she did not give me, and he is putting it in his mouth and smiling with his big, straight, sparkling teeth. I see all of this, but all I hear is the dirt crunching in my ears and *you ruined her* over and over. I don't know what it means, but I like the sound of it. It sounds like a movie, dramatic and important, and I am dramatic and important and worthy of having a movie made about me. There are people who will pay money to watch me get ruined. I am on the ground and can't get up and I feel like a movie star, the beautiful, tragic kind of movie star whose life ends too soon, whose death makes people remember them as brilliant.

James looks at me like I am something salvageable, like the something that got ruined is still there somewhere. He helps me up and says, "So you're not so straight," and I say, "No," even though I still didn't know what that means. And he says, "How are you feeling?" and I feel my feet leave the ground and the air in my lungs feels heavy and warm and full of mud, and he says, "I took some, too. I'll be like you soon."

The boys from the lunch table are shadows on the other side of the empty yard, watching and grinning like they know something I don't. They are drinking something brown out of a bottle and smoking something that does not smell like ciga- rettes. I am supposed to walk now but what I want more than anything in the world is to lie on the ground and look up and feel like I am at the bottom of something.

There are stairs a mile long that lead up to a deck with nothing on it. I hear my steps echo on the wood and I am waking up the whole neighborhood. There's a door that leads into a sci-fi kitchen, all shiny silver chrome with knobs and levers, the kind of kitchen in the magazines Mom buys, the kind of kitchen on the shows about rich people. The boys and Alex are here somewhere, but I do not see them. They are in the sink. They are hiding in cupboards. They are not in the refrigerator that is cold and full of boxes of takeout, a door full of condiments. There is a block of cheese with blue spots, and another that is round and dusty. I hold them in my hands and watch them melt through my fingers, staining my skin with the smell of feet that will never wash off.

James says, "What are you doing?" and I say, "Nothing," and he slaps my hand for handling the cheese, the fascinating cheese with names in different languages. He says I have to leave the kitchen. He says we can only be downstairs. It is pitch-black and I cannot hear the sound of my footsteps. Downstairs is his floor, his entire floor. Downstairs is his bedroom. I can make out a Ping-Pong table. My feet feel expensive carpet. My fingers do not feel a light switch.

He tells the boys to stay. He tells them we need to talk. They laugh and I laugh and I don't know what I'm laughing at but it is laughter and it feels better than the slap on my hand and the smell of the cheese and the cold steel refrigerator and the kitchen that is never cooked in. The boys sit on the couch and one of them farts and the other ones laugh. Alex opens drawers and touches things. James does not slap her hand. He is busy leading me into his room at the end of the hall. There is already music playing.

His walls are white brick. They are not real. They are the Pink Floyd album cover like my dad has. Painted, professional, commissioned by parents who are not here. The walls are dripping because I am on acid. He is not yet on acid. The tab is still on his tongue, dissolving, tasting like spit wad.

I'm thirteen and I'm on acid. He's fifteen and he will be on acid soon. I'm on his bed and under The Wall and listening to Pink Floyd. I do not know why James listens to music my dad likes. I do not know why I am looking at his stereo, the real kind, with different levels stacked on top of each other and blinking lights—green, red—with speakers as big as I am, playing Pink Floyd and reminding me of snow.

He is wearing a baseball cap and I want it off his head. It makes him look like a normal boy. I want his hat off because he is not that kind of boy. I would not be on my back like this for that kind of boy.

I pull off his baseball cap because I need him to be someone else. His hair is flat and straight like a girl's and falls into his eyes. He takes the hat out of my hand and puts it back on his head. He says, "Stop it," and I laugh, and I do it again and he grabs it again and I think it's a game but he does not, and he says, "Fucking stop it," and pins my wrist onto the bed, and I stop it. Then his tongue goes in my mouth and this is nothing like a first kiss is supposed to be.

Alex opens the door and says, "Can I use the phone?" James waves his hand and I can't tell if he's giving her permission or shooing her away, but she comes in and sits on his desk and picks up the phone and starts dialing. He takes off his hat because it is getting in the way of our faces and I know better than to ask why it's okay if he does it now but not when I wanted him to, and I cannot see what he looks like now because I'm closing my eyes.

Alex is on the phone talking to everyone she knows. I can feel her sitting on the desk next to the stereo blinking red and green, stop, go, and James's tongue is in my mouth and it tastes like something dusty, small, darting around and hitting my teeth like it's looking for a way to get inside me, a trapdoor, searching for something hidden and unlocked. And Alex is watching and telling everyone she knows, "Cassie's on the bed with James and they're slurping." She keeps saying "slurping" and it sounds like something ugly, and her cackle ricochets off the wall, the white bricks like the album cover, and it is too loud in here, it is too bright, and the slurping makes spit and the spit makes choking and I close my mouth and lock his tongue out and he says, "Get the fuck out, bitch," and I think he's talking to me, but Alex cackles and hangs up the phone and James says, "Turn off the lights," and she does, and "Close the door," and she does, and my teeth open and his tongue goes inside and I try to keep up but I have no idea what I'm doing and I'm scared because it's just me and him and I can't see anything but the green and red lights, and he's the only one who knows his way around here in the dark.

There's a mouth on mine and teeth scraping and I'm thinking of cheese. I'm thinking, why does expensive cheese stink? I'm thinking of my stubbly armpits that he's touching with his big hands. The sound of a zipper unzipping. The sound of Pink Floyd. And I'm thinking of snow. I'm thinking of driving fast through it, nothing but white shiny sometimes texture, patterns that shift and cackle because the sky is cloudy and the shadows are lying. And I'm wearing a white cotton bra that is not a bad-girl bra. He laughs. He says, "Is this a training bra?" and I look at the lights—red, green—and they tell me nothing about what I should answer. So I shrug as well as I can shrug with his body on top of mine and my right arm under his hot hand and my left arm not wanting to move at all and my shoulders cold and shuddering under Pink Floyd snow.

His fingers are inside me and I am trying to make my mouth move. I feel something that feels like sickness, something all through my body, like poison slowly filling me up. I don't know if my mouth is moving because I can't feel anything except the poison. There is something running in my brain. I cannot see it but I know it is coming. I can feel the pounding of the footsteps shaking everything. I hear pants unzipping, somewhere far away, and I don't know how long this is supposed to take but I hope it is fast because I want to go home. I want this feeling to stop. I want to give him what he wants and leave. I want to leave Alex out there with nothing to sit on. I want to leave the lunch-table boys to their farting and drinking. I want to leave James with his hat and his hair and his hands and his tongue and his wall and his stereo saying stop, go, directions that I do not hear.

Something in the other room crashes. He says, "Fuck," and runs out the door without zipping up his pants. I feel myself floating without the weight of him on my body. I hear the boys yelling and Alex cackling, and the CD is over and it's definitely time to go. I zip up my pants and put on my bra. I put on my shirt tangled in sheets. I walk out of the bedroom. I feel the ghosts of his fingers inside me.

There's a vase broken on the floor. James is yelling at the boy with the bottle in his hand. The other boys are burning each other with the hot metal on their lighters. Alex is sitting on the couch and looking at me like, *"Well?"*

"I'm going home," I tell her, and my voice sounds far away.

"No, you're not," she says.

"It's past my curfew," I lie.

"Did you guys do it yet?" she asks. I shake my head. "You have to stay a little longer. You have to stay until you do."

"I have to go home. I'll call you tomorrow."

I walk toward the door. James stops yelling and says, "Aren't you going to spend the night?"

The boys say, "Aren't you going to spend the night?"

Alex says, "Yeah," and I say nothing and all of them are looking at me like my life depends on what I do now, and everything is quiet and waiting and I want to run. "I have a curfew," I say. It is the closest thing I can say to something I'm not allowed to say, something not "No," not "I want to go," not "I don't want to be in your bed, not with your dripping walls, not with your hat on or off, not with you touching me, not with your fingers inside me or anything else from your body." I cannot say that. I cannot say anything close to true, just "I have a curfew" and James's hands are on my waist, pulling, his voice sick sweet: "Come on, baby." Alex's voice: "Wait." The lunch-table boys: "Cock tease." My voice tiny, inaudible: "I have a curfew," again and again, and his hands are pushing me away and his voice is hard: "What are you, a little girl?" Alex: "Jesus, Cassie." The lunch-table boys: "Cock tease. Little girl."

Yes, I am a little girl. I am nothing you want. I am leaving. I am walking out the sliding glass door that doesn't slide so well and across the dirt yard, down the hill, and across the train tracks, to the marina and through the shadows of masts of sailboats. The bench isn't comfortable. The bathroom is closed. There is nowhere to hide and stop and breathe. The lake is pockmarked with little tsunamis. Bells ring. Seagulls sleep.

I run up the hill away from the lake, past the rows of three-car garages, past the restaurant with the fifteen-dollar salads, past so many red and green lights. I run home to the apartment by the train tracks, darker even than the mansion by the lake. There are no leather couches, no smelly cheeses, no kitchens from magazines, no Ping-Pong tables, no Pink Floyd or expensive wall paintings. There is only black air and black shapes that make no sound. There is only my room and everything put exactly where it's supposed to be. There is my bed and my desk and my clothes and my books and a note from Alex still creased from elaborate foldings.

I will not sleep. I will sit here biting my nails until they bleed. I will look out the window at the black trees that used to be green. I will listen to the sounds the ghosts make. I will sit here in this dark and not remember anything. This is my place. Dark. A cave. Not a square house at the end of a gravel driveway. Not an island, rain-drenched, clouded with green. Those are not the skyscraper trees that talked behind my back. They do not whisper about the barefoot girl who is always alone. I am not the girl. She does not have a plastic shovel. It is not the weekend and my father is not home and my parents are not outside tearing up the earth and pretending to grow things. I am not wearing rubber boots or carrying a plastic shovel or asking Mom how to grow things, asking Dad how to grow things. No one is saying "Not now." No one is tearing up the earth. The trees aren't laughing.

I am not trying to sink in mud puddles. I am not telling the earth, "Take me." I am not dreaming of quicksand and earthquakes and monsters that steal me in the night. I am too old for pretend games, too old for Barbies, too old to take them into the forest and drown them in the stream, too old to tell them there is no one to save them and watch their still, serene faces covered with water, not scared, not fighting back, no screams coming out of their little painted mouths. There are no dolls. There is no girl. There are no parents building bonfires to destroy the things they uncover, no roots, no weeds, no blackberry bushes, no things with thorns, not left to burn, not left to grow unattended. I am not the girl with the fire or the shovel. This is not my forest. These are not my doll parts burning, not my legs, my arms, my head, my smooth pink torso. I am not watching them melt, not watching their perfect plastic faces turn grotesque. Smoke is not chasing me and making my eyes sweat. My eyes are not burning. I am not crying. I am not standing behind my mother and she is not facing the wall and she is not saying, "Smoke follows beauty."

Smoke follows beauty. Smoke follows beauty. Smoke follows beauty.

(FOUR)

"You're beautiful," Alex says. It's Friday night and we're in my bathroom. It's been a week since the disaster at James's house and, for some reason, she doesn't hate me. He thinks I'm a joke, but Alex says there's more where he came from. I don't know why she's being so nice to me. She is standing behind me in the bathroom and we are looking in the mirror. The fluorescent light reflects off the puke-green walls and makes us look like we're dead.

"I think you're the most beautiful girl I've ever known," she says.

I can see myself blush even through the thick foundation and powder I'm wearing. My eyes are lined in black and my lips are the color of blood. Alex showed me how to put on makeup and now I don't recognize myself.

"You really think I look good?" I say.

"You look hot. Fuck James. You could get a high schooler."

"Fuck James," I say, even though I felt like crying every time I saw him at school this week, with that other girl on his arm and that look on his face like, "Look what you're missing." It was only bearable because I had Alex, because she kept reminding the lunch-table boys how hot I am and, no, I am not a tease and, yes, I'm available.

"You should have stayed." She runs her fingers through my hair.

"I know," I say. If I had stayed, James wouldn't have had to invite over that other girl, the tall blond slut in ninth grade, the one with bigger boobs than me. She wouldn't have been the one to spend the night. She wouldn't have been the one to give him what he wanted. It was supposed to be me who did that. It was supposed to be me on his arm at school.

"We should move to Portland," she says as she pulls my hair back tight. I feel my whole face lift.

"Ouch," I say.

"Shut up," she says. "This looks good."

I look like I'm twenty-five.

"Why should we move to Portland?" I ask.

"I don't know. Because it's somewhere else. It's away from our parents. My brother's there. He's cool. You'd like him."

"My dad says the best bookstore in the world is in Portland."

"You are such a fucking nerd," she says.

"Your brother's in a gang against fat people," I respond, thinking it a witty comeback, but she grabs my hair even tighter and pulls my head back and looks at me in the mirror with a look on her face I have never seen.

"No he's not," she says slowly, her jaws clenched. "Don't ever say anything about my brother again."

"I'm sorry," I say.

She loosens her grip on my hair. "You know why he's in Portland?" she says.

"Why?"

"He left after he found my dad hanging in the basement."

I expect her to say more, to tell me that she's joking, but she just pulls my hair into a rubber band and it feels like my scalp is tearing off. "I'm sorry," I say again, but she looks like she didn't hear me. I don't say anything else because I don't want to make her mad again, but there's a picture in my head of a pale man with green hair and a rope around his neck.

"We should go soon," she says.

"Go where?" I ask.

"Portland. As soon as we get some money. What you have to do is steal a little out of your parents' wallets every day, not too much or they'll notice."

"What'll we do for money when we get there?"

"I don't know. My brother makes a lot of money. I could help him."

"What does he do?"

"Sells drugs."

"Oh," I say. She keeps pulling my hair tighter.

"He has a friend who could get you a job."

"Doing what?"

"Giving blow jobs."

I don't tell her I still don't know exactly what that is.

"You don't have to have sex with them," she explains. "That way, you keep your self-respect."

"What if I'm not good at it?"

"It doesn't matter. Old guys would pay a fortune to have you just look at their dick."

I don't want to look at an old guy's dick. I don't want to look at anyone's dick.

"I'm a genius," Alex says, and she takes her hands off my head. I look in the mirror. My hair is pulled back and gelled flat on my scalp. My face is a flat, uniform white, my eyes lined in thick black, my eyelids a dark purple. My lips are slimy, wet, and red.

There's a knock and I can smell my mom's cigarette even though there's a door between us. "Girls, are you ready for dinner?" she says.

"Yeah, Mom." I hear her feet shuffling away. "Do you want to stay for dinner?" I ask Alex. She looks at me like I'm an idiot.

"What do you think?"

"I don't know," I say. "My mom made spaghetti. Her spaghetti's pretty good."

"*My mom made spaghetti*," Alex mimics.

"She's making us have family night."

"Have fun with that," she says, and starts packing up her things.

"We could rent a movie and get some ice cream or something."

"Hell no," she says. "I want to get fucked up. I don't want to hang out with your parents in your shitty-ass apartment like a fucking baby. And neither should you."

"I have to."

"You don't *have* to do anything."

She throws her backpack over her shoulder and walks

out of the bathroom. I follow her to the front door. "Call me later," I say.

"Maybe," she says, and I would do anything to make her stay, to take back my stupid "I have to." I would walk out the door and go with her but my mom's standing in the living room and can see me, would follow me, would ask me where I'm going and why, and I wouldn't be able to tell her. I can't go. I have to stay, and my chest feels pulled apart so tight that there's nothing left in the middle. There's a hollow place where my heart should be, gutted and scraped and thrown out the door. I cannot breathe to fill it up. The emptiness feels like lead, like the heaviest thing in the world.

Alex doesn't look at me, just walks out the door without saying good-bye. I stand there looking at the door and trying to not pound my head against it, to not smash my fists into the hard wood until I bleed, until I crush my knuckles and the pain in my chest goes away.

"She's not staying for dinner?" Mom says from the living room.

I must act normal. I must pretend like everything's okay. "She had to go home and have dinner with her parents," I lie, even though all I know about her parents is that one of them is dead.

"Well, come on," says my mother, and I turn around. She

has changed out of the sweatpants she always wears. We're just eating at home tonight, but she's wearing makeup and a skirt and a ruffly blouse that's too small. Seeing her standing there like that, all dressed up in clothes that don't fit, makes me want to cry.

"Do you want help setting the table?" I say for some reason. She looks at me like I just gave her diamonds or a puppy.

"Yes," she says. "That would be nice."

As I set the table, I can see Dad on the porch through the sliding glass doors, still in his suit from work. He is standing with his leg propped up on one of the plastic chairs, looking out at Seattle. He started smoking cigars when we moved here, standing out on the porch with his chin in the air like he's posing for a magazine about rich businessmen.

"Get your father," my mom says.

"You do it."

"Cassie, just knock on the window."

I knock on the window and he doesn't hear, just keeps standing there like he's the king of the world. I knock harder and he turns around with smoke coming out of his face and I think this is what demons must look like. But he waves and puts out the cigar, and I think maybe tonight won't be totally awful. Maybe we'll actually act like a family. Maybe he won't hate us and maybe moving here was a good idea like Mom said.

The smell of cigar smoke follows Dad inside and makes everything taste like it. I can tell Mom's been drinking because she's talking too much, something about the talk show lady she watches every day and bulimic girls whose teeth fall out. "Jesus, Olivia," Dad says. "I'm trying to eat."

She stays quiet for about two seconds, then says, "How was school, Cassie?"

"Fine," I say.

"It's so nice that you've made friends so quickly."

"*Friend*, singular," I say.

"Be patient," she says. "You're just a little bit shy. But you're so pretty now, soon you'll have more friends than you know what to do with."

"The spaghetti's good, Mom," I say, even though it's cold and too salty.

Dad's looking at me with squinty eyes and a tight jaw and I try to ignore it and focus on eating, but the noodles won't stay on my fork and I'm just waiting for him to say something, to throw one of his temper tantrums that make us all shut up.

"What did you do to your face?" he says slowly. This is how it starts.

"Cassie and her new friend were just playing around with makeup," Mom says.

"Do you think that actually looks good?" he asks me with his eyebrows, which means I'm the stupidest piece of shit that ever lived.

"I don't know," I say to my plate of spaghetti.

"You are so naturally beautiful," says my mother. "You're so lucky not to need makeup like other girls."

"You look like a slut," says my dad.

"Honey," says my mom, picking up her drink, trying to suck out the little liquid that is left.

"What?" says my dad. "She does. What am I supposed to do, just pretend I don't see her face all painted up like a piece of cheap white trash?"

"It just sounds a little mean, is all," Mom says, looking at her drink like it let her down.

"Mean is not the same as honest, *dear*." He hates her.

Mom gets up to make another drink. I'm staring at my plate, trying to make the spaghetti move with the power of my mind. I want the noodles to tie themselves into knots, the intricate kind Boy Scouts know. I can see them moving, slithering around and making slurping noises, becoming bows, braids, nooses.

"Did you hear me?" he says.

"Yes," I say.

"Do you have anything to say?"

"No." I have nothing to say. I can barely hear him. I am making spaghetti move.

"How was work today, honey?" Mom says, and that is the cue to ignore me. Dad says, "Fine," and Mom says, "Don't be so modest, honey. You know all that hard work's going to pay off soon," and he's chewing like he wants to kill her. She starts talking about how we're going to have a big house and a swimming pool and a maid and now I want to kill her, too.

"How's that sound, Cassie?" Mom says, and I say, "Great," even though all I want is a small place where I can be alone and no one will look at me or talk to me or touch me. A tree house. A cave.

Everyone is chewing and not talking and the ice in Mom's glass clinks when she drinks and for some reason I think about how my dad and I have the same IQ, how I had to take that test answering stupid questions and putting triangles together, how Mom's always telling me, "You and your dad have the exact same IQ," like it's magic, like it's something to be proud of even though I did nothing to earn it. "It's hard work that gets you somewhere, not your IQ," Dad always says. "See where smarts got the rest of my family. A goddamned trailer park."

Mom's looking back and forth at me and Dad with this hopeful look on her face, waiting for some sign that this dinner is working, that it was worth her changing out of her sweatpants and doing her hair.

I say, "Excuse me," and go to the bathroom because I have to get out of the room with the silence and the spaghetti and the smell of cigars and the sound of Mom's ice cubes. I lock the door and look in the mirror and the green light brings out the bags under my eyes, makes my cheekbones look sharper. I don't look like a slut. That's not it. I look tough. I look like I could do anything. I could hurt people.

When I come out, Mom's standing outside of the bathroom door real close. She looks sad and I'm thinking maybe she's come to make me feel better. Maybe she's going to tell me to pack our things, we're leaving. Maybe she's finally had it. It can be just her and me. Somewhere new. Somewhere no one knows us.

"What?" I say.

"Your dad's going to do some work in the bedroom."

"So?" I say, trying to sound like I don't care, like I don't want her to do something like ask me how I feel.

She looks nervous and doesn't say anything. "What, Mom?"

"I just wanted to make sure . . . Well, you always seem to go to the bathroom after you eat. And the doctor on the talk show said—"

"Jesus, Mom, I'm not bulimic." That's what she's worried about. That's the only thing she's worried about.

She looks embarrassed, like she wishes she had said nothing, had just stayed sitting at the kitchen table all by herself with her drink and her ashtray and the remote control. All of a sudden, I am exhausted. I don't even care that it's Friday night and the only friend I have is mad at me, that I'm stuck at home with parents who think I'm a bulimic slut.

"Do you have plans for tonight?" my mom asks.

"No."

"Do you want to watch *A Chorus Line* with me?"

"Whatever," I say. I try to sound tough, but my voice cracks. When I think about it, watching cheesy musicals with my mom doesn't sound so bad. When I was little we used to choose characters out of movies and do all their parts. Sometimes I laughed so hard I couldn't breathe. The trick is being quiet enough so Dad doesn't get pissed off and tell us to shut up.

"I'll be Morales," I tell my mother.

"Who am I going to be?" she says. She always wants to be Morales, too. Because Morales is tough. Because she doesn't take shit from anyone.

"You can be that gay guy who breaks his ankle," I say.

"He doesn't have any good songs."

"Be the girl who sings 'Tits and Ass,'" I tell her.

"Me? No way," she says, but she seems flattered.

We stand there for a second, trying to not look at each other. "Mom?" I say, almost whispering, like I'm afraid someone will hear me, like Alex will hear me, even though I know she's already downtown by now, somewhere better with a cooler friend than me.

"Yes?" Mom says.

I am thinking about how warm it will be in my pajamas, the soft blue flannel with tiny pink sheep. I am wondering when the last time was that my head was in my mother's lap. I wonder if my head's ever been in my mother's lap.

"Will you make me some hot chocolate?" I say.

For a second, she smiles and her face doesn't seem so old. But then she is my mother again, with the double chin and the blotchy skin and the bags under her red, puffy eyes.

"Of course," she says, and takes a drag from her cigarette, and I decide that I will let her be Morales tonight.

(FIVE)

"I know him," Alex says.

"He's cool."

We're standing in line for tacos and the new guy's across the cafeteria slapping fives with the lunch-table boys.

"His name's Ethan," she says. "And he *drives*."

"How does he drive if he's only a ninth grader?"

"He flunked a grade."

"Oh."

One taco, Tater Tots, and a Diet Coke.

"He got kicked out of Rose Hill for selling weed," she says. All the guys are over there treating him like a celebrity. The girls are pushing their chests out, trying to get close and laughing whenever he says anything.

"Let's go talk to him," she says, and starts walking.

"No," I say, but she pretends not to hear me. I throw my food in the trash can even though I just got it. I cannot eat in front of boys, especially celebrity boys.

James the asshole has his arm around the slutty girl and he grins at me before he starts sucking on her ear, and she's looking at me and giggling like his dirty mouth on her ear makes her better than me. I look at the clock above the painting of the school's stupid wolf mascot and there are still fourteen minutes until class and I cannot wait that long to get out of here. Even sitting in class surrounded by people who hate me would be better than meeting this boy who's too cool and too old to talk to me.

"Hey, Ethan," Alex says to the new guy as he sticks his hamburger bun on the wall and everyone laughs.

"Oh, hey," he says. "I know you."

"My brother's David."

"Oh yeah. How is he?"

"Good," she says, but he doesn't hear her. He's already looking at me, and everyone's looking at him looking at me, and I want to disappear.

"Hello," he says, and extends his hand. I give him mine and let him shake it and his hand is big and warm and mine feels tiny and safe inside it. I know I am blushing but I look at him anyway and his lips look soft and wet and his eyes are big and brown. I let go of his hand and he smiles. I take a sip of my Diet Coke because I have to do something and it makes a slurping noise that is the loudest thing I've ever heard. Someone says something and he turns around and says something back, and pretty soon everyone's talking to someone and no one's talking to me. Alex is whispering something to Wes and his hand's on her leg and I'm just sitting here waiting for the bell to ring.

I'm looking at all the tables in the lunchroom—the gangsters next to us and nobody else brave or cool enough to sit next to them; the jocks and their skinny girlfriends; the Christian kids with their dorky clothes; the small table of Asians who are all somehow related and don't talk to anyone else. In the middle of the cafeteria is the ocean of normal kids who all look the same, who all look like the people I used to dream of being friends with, the girls who still have slumber parties, who pass notes and giggle in the halls. They are the boring kids, and among them are the even more boring gifted kids, the ones I was almost friends with, the ones who think about law school and med school, the ones who have never even tasted liquor, who are destined to do great things and still be boring. And I am sitting here, expelled from the world that welcomed me for just a few days. I can hear the gangsters talking about some rival who wronged them. I can hear James the asshole bragging about how high he got last night. I can hear the beautiful new guy talking about climbing on a freeway overpass and tagging the sign for Mercer Island.

"Yo, what's your tag?" asks Anthony, and Ethan takes a giant marker out of his pocket and writes it on the table: *Aleph*.

"What's that mean?" the guy says.

"*A*. It's Hebrew for *A*."

"A what?"

"*A*, the letter *A*. Like the first letter of the alphabet."

"That's cool."

"'Cause I'm the first, man. The best."

"Tight," says Wes, and they high-five. Everyone keeps talking and I keep drinking my Diet Coke and watching the clock and the wolf that doesn't look tough at all. Ethan keeps looking at me and smiling and I keep looking away because I can't tell if it's a nice smile or a laughing smile so it's best to pretend that I don't see it. He's writing something on a piece of paper and the bell rings and I stand up and he stands up and gives me the piece of paper. I put it in my pocket and say "Thanks" without looking at him and he says, "See ya," and walks away. I want to hit myself. *Thanks?* Are you supposed to say thanks when someone gives you a piece of fucking paper?

Alex says, "Bye," and she smiles at me like she knows something I don't. Everyone's gone except James the asshole and the slutty girl still making out on the bench, and I'm just standing here like an idiot with no friends. I start walking toward my classroom and I'm the only person in the whole school walking alone. I get to the door that says E&A, EXPANDED AND ADVANCED, the only class I have all day. While everyone else gets a new room and new teacher and new classmates every fifty minutes, I am stuck in here with the same losers and a teacher who hates me. I can see through the window everyone already sitting down and waiting attentively, and I consider for a moment making a run for it. But there is nowhere else to go.

Normal classes sit in rows. Gifted classes sit in circles. Gifted students are plain and dull and they used to think I was one of them. Now they don't talk to me and I don't talk to them. I keep quiet and do my work. I can see them all wondering what I'm doing here. They try to be sneaky when our papers come back, like they're not leaning over to look at my grades, like they're not pissed that I always get A's.

I sit in my seat next to Justin, the boy with the glasses and mildew-smelling coat. He's the only one who talks to me. Everyone hates him, too.

"Hi, Cassie," he says.

"Hi."

"Did you have a good weekend?"

"Fine."

"My mom put me on Ritalin." He's scratching something on his face.

"Why are you telling me that?"

"I don't know." He wipes his nose with the back of his hand. "What'd you do this weekend?"

"Hung out with some friends."

"Those ninth graders you're always talking to at lunch?"

"Maybe."

"They're not very nice."

"They're nice to me."

"No they're not."

"Don't talk to me," I tell him, and he obeys. He's the only person I talk to like this. I can't help myself. He just takes it, like it doesn't even hurt his feelings.

Mr. Cobb walks through the door and everyone turns even more attentive. They pick up their pens and open the notebooks that are already waiting anxiously at their desks. I take the piece of paper out of my pocket, breathe, and unfold it.

Yo Casy.

Why R U so shy?

Peace,

Ethan

p.s. I think your hot.

I am melting. I am wanting to tell Alex. I am wanting to shove this letter in James the asshole's face, in his slutty girl's face. I am going to explode.

"Why are you smiling?" Justin says.

"Don't fucking talk to me," I say too loud, and everybody looks at me like I just pissed on the floor.

"Cassie, you're this close to detention," Mr. Cobb says with his white, skinny fingers held up like tweezers, and the gifted boys snicker and the gifted girls roll their eyes like they always do.

"Sorry," I say, but I'm not. I have this note in my hand and that's all that matters. What matters is the coolest guy in school thinks I'm hot. I stare at the letter, looking for more clues, but all I see is my misspelled name and the incorrect form of "your" so I take a pen out of my bag and make it perfect. The letter is perfect and the boy who drives wants me.

"Did everyone finish *Romeo and Juliet*?" Mr. Cobb asks, and everyone says yes. A couple of girls who went to private school together roll their eyes again, and I want to tell them it would be more efficient if they never stopped rolling their eyes, if they just kept them rolling and rolling until they rolled right out of their heads and I could step on them and smash them like grapes.

One of them whines, "We read that *two years* ago."

Mr. Cobb says, "Then you'll be that much ahead of the curve," and that seems to satisfy them. "Some of us haven't read any Shakespeare yet," he says, and everybody looks at me like I'm responsible for this remedial assignment.

"We're going to break up into groups of two to analyze and perform a scene for the class," he says. Everyone starts squealing and fighting for partners while smelly Justin and I just sit there because we're the only ones no one wants.

He looks at me and says, "You want to be my partner?"

"Whatever."

Mr. Cobb tells us to move our chairs together and discuss our scene, and Justin is already turned to the page with the kissing.

"You be Juliet and I'll be Romeo," he says.

"You be Tybalt and I'll be Mercutio," I tell him.

"But you die," he says.

"And you kill me."

(SIX)

"Home sweet home,"
Alex says, and it smells like smoke and something rotting. The front door closes with a bang and she throws her coat on the floor, onto a pile of other coats and half-emptied shopping bags. There is a frozen pizza in one of them that appears to be fully thawed. The paper bag is dark with moisture and there's a puddle around it.

"This way," she says, and leads me into the living room. There is stuff piled everywhere and I can hardly see the floor. The room is hot and the air feels damp, like someone has been taking a shower for months.

"This must be Cassie," says a raspy voice coming from the couch. I did not notice the woman lying there with hair and clothes as black as the leather. Her lips are red with lipstick and her eyes are painted dark and something about her reminds me of a cat. A thin, lanky, sleepy cat.

"Aren't you supposed to be at work, Lenora?" says Alex.

"I'm home sick," says the woman, faking a cough and laughing a deep laugh. She is the most beautiful woman I have ever seen.

"Yeah, right," Alex says to the woman. "Let's go downstairs," she says to me. I nod and follow even though I want to keep listening to this cat-woman purring in her low voice.

"Cassie," the woman says, and I turn around. She sits up and pats the space next to her on the couch. "Come talk to me for a minute."

I look at Alex and her face is angry, but I go and sit by the woman anyway. The couch is warm where her legs were and I sink into it. Something smells familiar.

"My daughter tells me you're smart," the woman says, looking into my eyes so hard I have to look away. I cannot believe this is Alex's mother. I cannot believe this is anyone's mother.

"Kind of," I say. "Not really."

"I thought she was going to be smart. But she turned out just like her brother." She picks up a glass from the coffee table and swirls the ice around, just like my mom does.

"Did she tell you about her trip to the loony bin?" the woman says.

"Very funny," says Alex, who does not look amused. She is still standing by the stairs.

"Her crazy brother took her along with him to skin some cats."

"Shut the fuck up," Alex says.

"You shut up, you little brat," she says, then yawns and closes her eyes as she stretches her long body, arching her back and lengthening her neck like she wants to be scratched. "I'm telling a story," she says, and takes a sip of her drink. She lights a cigarette with her eyes closed and I sink deeper into the couch.

"We took them both to get fixed," she continues, opening her eyes halfway, her fuzzy glance settling somewhere in the direction of Alex. "What'd they call your brother?"

"I don't know, Lenora. What'd they call him?"

"A sociopath. Doesn't that have a nice ring to it?" She takes a drag from her cigarette and leaves a perfect red halo around the filter. "And this one"—she motions to Alex, blowing smoke in her direction—"they said it was too early to tell."

The room is silent and Alex is smiling and wide-eyed like she's crazy. I don't want to believe the story, but I do. Lenora is staring at me like she can see right through me, like she knows everything about me, and I want to disappear.

She laughs a raspy laugh. "I bet your family's nice and normal, huh, pretty girl?"

"I don't know."

She leans back on the couch and ashes her cigarette on the floor.

"Parents still married."

"Yes."

She takes another drag and blows it out slowly. I look at Alex leaning against the banister, trying to tell her with my eyes that I want to go, but she doesn't look at me. She keeps staring at her mother, like I'm not even there.

"How nice," Lenora says, and then turns so she is facing me. Her leg touches mine and I feel lightning surge through me, something warm inside, outside, spreading, everywhere. She looks into my eyes and I feel my face turn hot and everything solid inside me turn to thick liquid.

"I should have had a girl like you," she says. She raises her hand and slides her palm down my cheek. I close my eyes and feel the warmth expanding. "Sensitive."

"Let's go," says Alex, almost shouting, and I open my eyes. She is not smiling. She is walking over. She is behind me, tugging on my shoulder. "Let's *go.*"

I get up. I follow her to the stairs. My feet move my body, but part of me is still on the couch, still warm and melting.

I look back and Lenora's lying down with her eyes closed, the cigarette dangling from her red lips, like I was never even there. The air is hazy with smoke and dust and setting sun through dirty windows, and I have a sudden urge to curl up beside her, to press against her, to absorb her. I want to wear her black clothes and lipstick. I want to scare girls like me.

But I let Alex pull me downstairs to the cold, unfinished basement. The walls are concrete and lined with piles of boxes, rusted bikes, and other broken things. Alex opens a door to a small, carpeted room with a stained mattress on the floor and graffiti the color of blood on the wall. "This was my brother's room," she says, matter-of-factly. She points to a broken light fixture on the ceiling. "And that's where—drumroll, please—my dad hung himself."

I look at her in disbelief. "Are you serious?"

"Yeah. Pretty cool, huh?"

No, I am thinking. *That is the least cool thing I have ever heard.*

"When?" I ask because I don't know what else to say.

"I don't know," she says, kicking a broken skateboard. "A couple years ago."

"That's when your brother left?"

"Yeah. He just left him up there and packed up his shit and was gone. The funniest part is he left a note right next to the suicide note. It said, 'Dad's hanging in the basement. I'm leaving. Bye.' What a weirdo."

"What'd the note say?"

"I just told you."

"No, the suicide note."

"Oh, that. I don't know. I never read it."

Alex keeps kicking the skateboard and I want to grab her and make her stop. I want to grab the skateboard and hit her with it. But she would probably just laugh. Even if her jaw were broken and she was covered in blood, she'd just smile at me with her big crazy eyes and make me feel like there is nothing I can do to hurt her.

"Did you really do that with the cats?" I finally say.

"What do you think?" she says, smiling.

If I say no, she'll laugh at me. If I say yes, she'll do something worse. So instead I say, "Let's get ready to go," and she smiles like she knows exactly what I was thinking.

The bathroom smells like mildew and old piss and there are strands of green hair stuck everywhere. A box of tampons is spilled on the floor and the towels look like they haven't been washed in months. I am tracing the outline of my lips with bloodred pencil and I can see Alex behind me in the reflection. She is sitting on the toilet, peeing, and her thighs are covered with bruises.

"What happened?" I ask her.

"To what?" she says, wiping herself.

"To your legs?"

She laughs at me like I'm a stupid child. "Wes just likes it rough."

"Likes what rough?"

"Sex, stupid," she says. "But you wouldn't know anything about that, would you? Not Cassie, the sweet little virgin."

I don't say anything. I turn around and start curling my eyelashes.

"How much money did you steal?" she says as she gets up and flushes the toilet. She grabs a pair of fishnets that were hanging on the doorknob.

"Huh?" I say.

"For Portland, dummy. So we can move to Portland."

"Oh," I say. "I didn't think you were serious about that."

"Of course I'm fucking serious," she says, her voice hard. She's looking at me like she wants to kill me. "Are *you* serious? Or are you a fucking chicken?"

"I'm serious," I say.

"Because I can find someone else to come with me."

"No," I say. "I'm serious."

"Then start getting some money. And have a bag packed so you're ready whenever it's time."

"How will we know it's time?"

"I'll figure that out," she says. She sprays some hair spray and it makes my eyes burn.

"We're ready," she says, and it's time to go.

Lenora is passed out when we leave, so Alex steals a pack of her cigarettes and a bottle of vodka, just puts them in her backpack like it's no big deal, like she's not even afraid of getting caught. We walk to the lake and it's freezing. I drink fast so I'll get warm, so I don't have to think about that house and the things that happened in it, so I won't be scared of where we're going.

"My half sister's moving in next week," Alex says, her voice torn by the shot she just drank.

"How old is she?"

"Eighth grade."

"Is she cool?"

"She's all right."

"Why's she moving here?"

"Her dad's fucking her," she says, and the vodka gets stuck in my throat, gagging me, pulling everything inside me out.

"We have the same mom," she says. "But Sarah's dad was some guy my mom had an affair with so my dad made my mom get rid of her."

"Oh," I manage, trying not to throw up, trying to make sense of what Alex just said.

"Now the stupid social workers say she has to come live with us even though we don't want her."

"Oh," I say again because I can't think of anything else. I'm not anywhere near drunk, but my stomach feels like it's full of poison, like there's a fist inside moving it around. I am doing everything I can to keep from puking. I am clenching my teeth, my fists. I am walking fast. I am thinking of summer and beaches and sun on my face.

We crest the hill and see Lake Washington, dark and choppy, Seattle sparkling behind it. We get closer and can see the shadowed group of boys, none of whom I recognize.

"Who are those guys?" I ask.

"High schoolers."

I want to turn around. The vodka's not working. I drink more and it's still not working.

"Where's Ethan?" I ask.

"Right there." Alex points and he is lit by moonlight, standing on top of a bench in his baggy pants and giant sweatshirt, balancing on it like a tightrope. We get closer and I can hear the other boys cheering him on. I feel something in my stomach that is not nausea, a pleasant, heavy numbness. The fear is not gone, but it is somehow softer.

A tall boy with a pierced lip turns around and looks us up and down. "What do we have here?" he says. Ethan hops off the bench and smiles and the numbness turns to melting.

"Hi," he says to me, ignoring Alex. "I'm glad you came."

"Yeah," I say.

"Do you want to sit down?" He motions toward the bench covered with his dirty footprints. I sit and he sits next to me and everyone else sits and soon we are all in a circle, and Alex is passing around the bottle of vodka and it is getting emptier and emptier and I am suddenly very angry. I am furious. *That is* our *vodka*, I want to tell her. They are drinking it and it will be gone and there won't be enough for me.

Everyone's talking except me. I drink extra when the bottle comes around so I won't think about the fact that I'm not talking. It does not take long for me to get drunk enough so my mind does not have to be here anymore. I am thinking of tropical islands and warm water and I feel okay even though I'm sitting here with a bunch of high schoolers and I haven't said anything in thirty minutes. I haven't been paying attention to what anyone's been saying because I've been somewhere else, and all of a sudden everyone but me is up and Alex is screaming because the guys are carrying her over to the embankment and threatening to throw her into the lake.

"Hey," says Ethan, and I think he's going to save her, although I wouldn't mind if he didn't. And I'm surprised at this thought and I look around to make sure no one heard it, but everyone's laughing and not at me. "It's time to go," he says, and he's the boss so they let her go. She's laughing like she was in on the joke, but I don't think she was. Ethan gets up and I am suddenly very cold. They all grab their backpacks and skateboards and I'm relieved but feeling pathetic, and I want to crawl into a little ball and hide in a cave and never come out, not until I'm old and all of this is done with.

I am sitting on the bench, and Alex is standing by the water, and everyone else is walking away. Ethan hangs back and sits back down next to me. "It was nice seeing you tonight," he says with his soft lips and long eyelashes, like he didn't even notice that the only thing I said all night was "yeah."

"You too," I say.

"It'd be nice to hang out just you and me sometime," he says, and the warm, spreading feeling comes back. "I'd like to get to know you better. Maybe you wouldn't be so shy if it was just you and me."

"Yeah," I say, even though I doubt it. I will never be able to talk to him. But I can do things other than talk.

"I have to run," he says. "Can I have a hug?"

"Okay," I say, and I cannot remember the last time someone hugged me.

There are arms around me, a hard chest against mine, hands on the small of my back, breath in my ears. This is when I'm supposed to put my arms around his neck, when I'm supposed to put my face close to his. This is when I'm supposed to kiss him, when he's touching me and his warmth is getting inside my clothes. I'm supposed to do it now or he won't be interested later. I must kiss him because what he wants is not my voice. He doesn't really want to talk. He doesn't really want to get to know me better, not really know me, not get inside my head where the hidden things are. I must kiss him because what he wants is my mouth, my hands on his back, my body, close, closer. I must turn my head, feel his breath on my face, move my lips to his mouth. Open. Tongue in. Out. Close my eyes. They like it when you close your eyes.

"*Damn*, girl," he says, licking his lips.

"What?" I say, smiling, my head cocked to one side. I am looking him straight in the eye. I am a different person. I am not scared. I know what he wants.

"Just *damn*."

"C'mon, man," someone yells from across the street. The others are laughing their always-laughs that never seem to be directed at anything.

"I gotta go," he says, backing away and looking me up and down.

"See you later," I say. I am still looking in his eyes. Brown. Shallow.

"Definitely," he says, then, "Mmm," and this must be what it feel like to be a piece of meat, to be wanted by someone hungry. This is all I have to do. This is easy. I am delicious.

Alex and I walk away from the lake. She has a big grin on her face but isn't saying anything and I'm just waiting for her to tell me I fucked up somehow, that I looked like a fool in front of the high school boys. All of a sudden, she stops walking and looks at me and puts her hands on my shoulders.

"I can't believe you did that," she says, smiling at me like I've made her proud.

"What?" I say.

"Just kissed him like that."

"Why?" I am smiling now, too. I have done something right.

"What happened to the sweet little virgin Cassie?" She is laughing.

"I don't know." I laugh back. I am giddy.

"She's gone," Alex says.

"Yeah," I say. We are running down the street now. We are laughing so hard we're screaming.

"The fucking bitch is gone," Alex says.

"Bye-bye," I say.

"Bye-bye, Cassie," she says.

"Bye-bye."

(SEVEN)

Sarah is nothing like

I expected. She's not beautiful, but she's something close to pretty. She's small and blond and quiet and looks younger than I do, like something made her stop growing. She's not small like I am, not like a miniature woman, but small like a large child, as if her body's not strong enough to hold her and there's nothing between her skin and her bones. Everything that should be solid is brittle. You could break her in half with your hands.

She gets this blank look on her face, like she's frozen, like all life has been sucked out of her. She doesn't even blink, just sits there looking out into space like she thinks that's where she belongs. You could blow on her and she'd fall over and crumble into a million pieces.

"Sarah," I say. She doesn't move.

"Sarah," I say again. She is sitting on the edge of Alex's bed, looking out the window even though it's all steamed up and all you can see are drippy blobs of color, green where the trees are, gray for the sky.

"Sarah!" Alex yells. "Wake up, you fucking freak."

Sarah blinks and looks at us. "What?" she says, like nothing's wrong, like she doesn't even know she was a zombie for three minutes.

Alex's room is as messy as the rest of the house, full of dirty dishes, piles of clothes, and old, ripped magazines. The floor is covered but the walls are completely blank. There are no posters, no photos, no cutouts of rock stars or actors. It's as if this is a garbage dump, a storage room, a place to pile unwanted things, instead of a teenage girl's bedroom. We're sitting on the floor, passing a joint around, and we want something stronger.

"Doesn't that nasty kid in your smart class take Ritalin?" says Alex.

"I love Ritalin," says Sarah, and her face lights up. It's the most animated I've seen her.

"Call him," says Alex.

"I don't have his number," I say, which is a lie because we've been partners for every single group project. As much as I want to get high and as much as I hate him, there's something that makes me want to keep Alex away from Justin.

"Talk to him on Monday, then."

"I will," I say.

"What are we going to do?" says Sarah as she twirls her hair around her fingers. Her hair is patchy all over because she pulls it out. She doesn't even know she's doing it. You can't really tell it's like that when she wears it up, but right now her hair is down and she looks like a cancer patient.

It's Saturday and Alex doesn't know where her mom is. There's no food in the house, so I brought some over. She's on her fourth peanut butter and jelly sandwich. Sarah is gnawing absentmindedly on a piece of sandwich meat she has wrapped around her finger.

"I am so fucking bored," says Alex, and Sarah and I say, "Me too," in unison.

"We need money," she says, and Sarah and I nod our heads. We sit in silence for a while, thinking about money and getting high. I am thinking about Ritalin. I am trying to guess what it could do, why something so great could be a kid's prescription. My stomach turns over and my body tingles. Of course he will give it to me. He probably won't even make me pay. I will have an endless supply of something new to feel.

"Oh, shit," says Alex. "I have the best fucking idea."

"Here you go, girls," the old lady says as she hands me a five-dollar bill. I put it in the manila envelope.

"Would you like a receipt?" Sarah asks. "For tax purposes." We stole a receipt pad from the office supply store down the street. We thought of everything.

"Oh no, girls, that's fine," the lady says. "What would I do with another piece of paper?"

We say our good-byes and thank yous and Sarah adds a "God bless you" and I think I'm going to burst with laughter as we speed-walk around the corner to where Alex is waiting for us. As soon as we get out of sight of the old lady's house, I am laughing so hard I think I'm going to pee my pants and Sarah's practically on the ground and she keeps saying, "I can't breathe, I can't breathe," and then gulps for air, and I put my arm around her shoulders and focus on my bladder.

Alex emerges from behind a van. "What's so funny?" she says, like she's angry.

"You should have seen that lady," Sarah says.

"Sarah blessed her," I say, and we're laughing again and Alex does not look happy.

"How much did you get?"

"Five dollars," I say, and suddenly things don't seem so funny because Alex is all business and there's a scowl on her face like we've done something very wrong.

"We need more."

"Oh, lighten up," Sarah says, and now no one is laughing. Now everything is heavy and ruined.

"Don't talk back to me," says Alex.

"Why not?"

"Because I'll hurt you."

"Bullshit."

"You don't believe me?"

"No."

They stare each other down and I want to be anywhere but here. Sarah looks weird, like she's someone else, possessed, like she could die right now and not care. Alex looks like she could kill her.

I could leave and no one would notice. I could just walk away.

"Hit me," Sarah says, looking Alex straight in the eyes.

"You want me to hit you?"

"Yeah, hit me."

They stare at each other while Alex considers this. I am quiet. I look up at the tops of trees like I see something interesting. I must pretend I'm invisible. I must pretend nothing's wrong. My body's tense, solid, like my petrified muscles are the only thing keeping Alex and Sarah from killing each other. My brain is black space, empty, with one line of tiny white writing, barely visible, white words against black, silently repeating, *Please stop please stop please stop.*

Alex rolls her eyes and starts walking. "I'm gonna hit you when you don't want it," she says.

"Whatever," Sarah says, and we follow Alex to the next house. I can breathe now. I am glad we are moving. I am glad we are in a single-file line, saying nothing, not looking at each other. I am glad we are pretending nothing happened.

A mother with two crying young children gives us a twenty just to make us go away. An old man gives us seventy-six cents and invites us to come in and see his collection of World War II memorabilia. A woman with a million cats gives us a five. A thirty-something guy in a stained white undershirt gives us nothing, but tells us we're pretty and says he'll give us some whiskey if we stick around. I consider it, but Sarah starts walking.

We knock on the door of a small house with a yard that looks like it was beautiful until recently. The hedges betray perfectly trimmed angles, fallen leaves litter the overgrown grass, and the skeletons of various flowers line the side of the house. I can hear movement inside and someone talking. A frail old woman opens the door and smiles when she sees us. A strange odor seeps out of the house, like something way too sweet.

"Oh, hello," she says, like she's been waiting for us.

"Hello, ma'am," Sarah says and starts the speech, but the lady keeps looking back and forth at us with the big grin on her face like she's not even listening. Sarah gets to the part about the animals when the lady interrupts her.

"Come in, come in," she says. "George and I were just sitting down for dinner."

"We don't want to impose," Sarah says.

"Honey, the more the merrier," says the lady. "We love company, don't we, George?" she calls behind her into the house, but no one answers.

As we enter, the smell is overwhelming. My eyes start to water and Sarah coughs. The lady is saying something about having no grandchildren, but I can't hear her because I'm looking around the house at every single table and windowsill and countertop covered with vases full of molding, dead flowers, giant bouquets like the kind people send after someone dies. The table is set for two but no one is there. A small pile of saltines is on one of the plates next to a half-eaten can of tuna.

"Now what were you saying about gerbils?" the lady asks.

"We're raising money to buy them," I say. "For our science class."

"Oh," the lady says. She looks around the room nervously,

as if searching for gerbils or cash or something that will help us. "I think—" the lady says, but doesn't finish her sentence. She is digging through the pockets of her polyester pants.

"It's okay," Sarah says. "If you can't—"

"No," the lady says. "I want to help you." She walks into the living room, over to the couch, picks up a purse, and starts rummaging through it.

"I think we've actually reached our goal," Sarah says, looking at me with a sadness in her eyes that makes her suddenly look very old. "I think we're done fund-raising, so we're going to go now."

"No, wait," the lady says. "I know I have some money for you." There is a panic growing in her voice. My eyes search for something to look at, anything but her. I look at the table. There are flies on the tuna. There is mold on the saltines.

"It was nice meeting you, ma'am," I say, already walking toward the door. "We'll see our way out."

"No, wait," she says again. "George, see if you have any money for these nice girls."

I open the door and suck in fresh air. I look behind me and Sarah is taking a twenty-dollar bill out of our manila envelope. She places the money under the plate that holds the lady's awful dinner. The lady is still in the living room, rummaging through her purse and saying, "No, wait," over and over, asking George to help her. Sarah meets my eye and starts walking, and I love her more than I've ever loved anyone.

We walk quickly to where Alex is waiting. We say nothing. We are closer to each other than we need to be, our shoulders and hands bumping.

Alex is standing around the corner smoking a cigarette. "How much do we have so far?" she says. Sarah hands her the manila envelope and Alex counts the money while we stand there, our shoulders just barely touching. "Fifty-two seventy-six," Alex says. "That's enough for some tacos and weed and acid."

We go to the arcade and meet Purple Haze and I don't sleep until tomorrow.

(EIGHT)

We're driving away from school in Ethan's '87 Honda Civic and I'm waving like I'm in a parade. People are gathered around to watch us go. There should be streamers, balloons, a big band playing. I am fighting the urge to honk the horn.

I am riding in the front seat of a car with the coolest guy in school. That makes me the coolest girl in school.

Alex is waving with that smile on her face like *I know what you're going to do*, and Sarah looks sad and mousy like *Don't leave me alone with her*, and James the asshole is there with a look on his face that says *I am such a dumb-ass*, and I want to yell out the window, "Look what you're missing!"

"What do you want to do?" Ethan asks me when we get

away from school. Suddenly, his car doesn't seem so spectacular. I notice the faint smells of hamburgers and mildew. We are driving through quiet residential streets.

"I don't know," I say. I want to keep driving. I want to drive by every single person I know. I want them to squint their eyes and look in the window and see that it is me.

"Are you hungry?" he says.

"No."

"I'm fucking starving."

"There's food at my house. My mom'll be asleep until five." I don't know why I say this. It seems like the right thing to say.

"Cool," he says, and I tell him where to go.

I want to keep driving. I want to go back and get Sarah. I don't want to go to my house and watch him eat. I don't want him in my room where he can see the chair I sit in by the window when I'm alone, where I sleep, where I lie on my back and look at the ceiling. I don't want to be alone with him.

This is what he meant by "I want to get to know you better." This is the "alone time." This is when we pass a joint back and forth and I let him talk and let him think I am interested in what he's saying. We are talking about the things you are supposed to talk about before you have sex.

He tells me: "My father is an artist, but I don't live with him. My mother is an accountant and amateur bodybuilder."

I tell him: "My father does something with computers. My mother does nothing."

It is the middle of the afternoon and my mother is sleeping. She does not know we are here, in my bedroom, on my bed. She does not know his hand is under my shirt and rubbing while he talks. He does not know that I feel nothing.

I have never met a bodybuilder, but I've seen them on TV. I am wondering what Ethan's mother looks like, if she's the kind of woman who looks like a man.

"My father lives in Israel," he says. "I'm gonna live with him when I graduate."

What's so special about Israel? I want to say, but I don't.

"My mom's a gentile, so according to Jewish law, I'm not Jewish. I don't know why my father married a fucking gentile." He says this as he's unbuttoning my gentile pants, as he slides his hand into my gentile underwear.

This is what I know about him: He likes skateboards and hamburgers (no cheese; not kosher). He does not like vegetables or school. He does like beer and pot and nitrous oxide and ketamine.

What he knows about me is my first name, how old I am, and that I live in this apartment building. He knows that my mom sleeps like the dead in the late afternoon, that we have bulk quantities of snacks, that my door locks, that I'm a good kisser, that I let him do anything he wants. He knows that my underwear and bra are pink and lacy. He does not know about the old white cotton bras and underwear hidden in the back of my drawer. He does not know my face without makeup.

He knows what it feels like to be on top of me, that I don't move, that I am small and thin and pliable, that my breasts are the perfect size for his hand.

I am thinking, *This is supposed to be special.* I am thinking, *Everybody's lying about this being special.* I am strangely not scared. All of this seems vaguely familiar, like I've seen it in movies, like I've seen myself doing it. I wonder why I can hardly feel anything else, how I can know that it hurts but not even feel it, how I don't even have to be here, how I can drift away to somewhere else, float up to the ceiling and watch how ridiculous we look: him thrusting into me like his life depends on it; me lying there looking like I'm wood, something hard and unbendable, when really I'm nothing, when really I'm just skin wrapped around fog.

"Does it hurt?" he asks me.

"It's okay," I say.

"Does it feel good?" he asks me.

"Yeah," I say. I am lying. It feels like nothing. I wish he

would stop talking. I wish he would stop making me speak. It is hard to speak when I'm on the ceiling, in the corner. It makes me have to come back down, feel his weight on top of me, feel him hard inside me, punching my insides. I come down long enough to say what he wants to hear, then float away again. It is not difficult, this flying from place to place. It is like I was born knowing how to do it.

"Oh, shit, I'm gonna come," he says, and I hear him and my ears bring me back to the bed just in time to feel him shudder, hear him groan. He holds his breath and the world pauses and I feel like I'm holding the whole thing up with my skinny arms and bent knees, my legs spread wide open, then everything lets go and he falls on top of me and I sink into the mattress until I am nothing.

He lies like that for a while, like he's dead, and I think for a moment that he is. I would not be traumatized if he died on top of me, his shrinking, shriveling dick still inside me. Anything could happen and it would not matter.

He rolls over and digs through the pockets of his pants on the floor. He puts a cigarette in his mouth, gives me one. I open the window, light some incense and put the jar I use as an ashtray on the bed between us. I lie back down next to him, cornered between the wall and the ashtray. We barely fit. I feel too naked. He rolls onto his side and faces me, puts his arm around me. He kisses my shoulder, my neck, my jaw, my ear, making annoying cooing noises as he does it. I want him to stop. I want to crush my cigarette on his eyelid. I would rather he keep fucking me for the rest of the night than lie here staring at me and tracing my ribs with his fingertips, acting like what happened meant something.

"That was beautiful," he says, and kisses me softly on the mouth and all I can do to keep from throwing up is squeeze my eyes shut, lift the cigarette up to my mouth, tighten my lips, suck, blow, put my arm back down. Over and over I do this, visualizing the smoke becoming solid inside my body, until the cigarette filter is melting and I put it out in the ashtray.

I make myself move to get up to go to the bathroom. I make my body turn and climb over him, my feet walk, my arms pull myself into my bathrobe. His eyes follow me, heavy-lidded, like they're just moving because they need something to do.

"Hey," he says.

"Yeah?" I am backing out the door.

"I love you," he says, and it sounds ridiculous. Everything about him is ridiculous: the messy hair; the forest of zits on his chin; the thin, pathetic attempt at a mustache; the white thigh; the penis laying against it, shriveled and small with the condom still on.

"I love you, too," I say because it's the only thing I can

think of, because it's the only thing you're allowed to say when someone says they love you first. Maybe that's all love is—one person saying it because they think they're supposed to and the other person feeling too guilty to say anything else—and everyone's delusional who believes it's anything like Shakespeare, because Romeo and Juliet were just crazy and horny and the same ages as me and Ethan. Maybe this is all love is and all it will ever be—boys fucking girls and pretending it's love, girls getting fucked and pretending they like it, saying "I love you, too," and wanting to throw up.

I open the door and run to the bathroom. I lock the door and hug the toilet. My mouth is open and watering and the drool is going drip, drip, drip. I wait and nothing comes. I am empty inside so nothing comes.

I brush my teeth. I splash cold water on my face. I pee and wash myself with a wet washcloth. I want him to leave so I can take a shower. I want to take the hottest shower I have ever taken.

When I get back to my room, he is sitting up and pulling his shorts on. Something on his face is wrong.

"Hey," I say.

"Hey." He is not looking at me.

"What's wrong?" I say, trying to sound calm, but all of a sudden I can't breathe. I have done something wrong. I let him do everything he wanted, but I missed something. I did everything but it wasn't enough. He is not happy with me. I have done something wrong.

He looks at his lap, searching for the right words. Finally, he says, "You didn't bleed," in a small voice. He does not seem angry, but I don't know what else he could be.

"What do you mean?" I say.

"Virgins are supposed to bleed," he says, and I realize he is pouting, looking at the white sheets like they let him down, searching for blood like it's some kind of trophy.

"What are you talking about?" I have done something wrong but I don't know what it is. I am trying not to fall apart.

"You're a virgin, aren't you?"

"Yes." Of course I'm a virgin. Why wouldn't I be a virgin?

"Thirteen is pretty young to not be a virgin."

"I *am* a virgin." Of course I'm a fucking virgin. My hands ball up into fists and my eyes get watery and I can't make the tears stop. It feels like the world is ending, like someone has found the perfect way to kill me, like some hole inside me has opened up and all my guts are falling out. I am trying not to shake. I cannot let him see me cry. Why am I crying? It's only blood, the absence of blood. I let him do everything he wanted. That's what matters. He is not mad. He is not mad at me.

He looks at me, repentant, like he suddenly understands that he misspoke. But that is not it. I don't know what it is, but that is not it at all.

"I'm sorry," he says. He pats the space next to him on the bed. I sit down. I breathe. I count to ten. I push the feelings away.

"It's just that I always thought girls were supposed to bleed their first time. I was just wondering because, like, you didn't bleed and there's, like, supposed to be that thing that breaks."

"Not all the time," I tell him. I am breathing. I know this. I read it in the book Mom gave me to teach me about sex. Sometimes it breaks from other things. Horseback riding. Accidents.

I pick one. I say, "Horseback riding."

"What?"

"I used to ride horses. That's what did it."

"Oh," he says. He looks skeptical.

"All the bouncing," I tell him.

"Okay."

I don't care if he thinks I wasn't a virgin. I don't care if he thinks I'm a slut, if he thinks I've fucked a million boys before. All I want is for him to stop talking about this. I want nothing, silence. I want no memory, no feeling, no one, nothing inside me.

Ethan finishes dressing while I look out the window at the wall of green trees that separates us from the next apartment building. He hands me my clothes and I just look at them sitting in my lap. Getting dressed seems like the most difficult thing I will ever have to do. Then I hear my mom's bedroom door open, her slippered feet padding across the living room floor, and I throw my clothes on and smooth down my hair, and Ethan is up and out of my room and I follow him to the front door and my mom is sitting on the couch and turning on the TV and she looks at us and says, "Oh, hello," and I say, "Mom, this is Ethan," and she says, "Nice to meet you, Ethan," and he says, "You too," and she says, "Ethan, would you like to stay for dinner?" and he says, "Thank you, but I gotta be someplace." I walk him to the door and he kisses me on the cheek, lingering too long so I can smell his hot, stale breath.

"You're my girl, right?" he says softly.

"Right," I say. What else would I be? You're the most popular guy at school and I'm nobody. I will keep letting you fuck me until you get tired of it, until you find someone better to fuck.

He backs out the door batting those eyelashes I thought were so sexy when I first met him. Now I want to pluck them out one by one. I close the door behind him and my skin feels like spiders and snakes and every disgusting thing imaginable is crawling all over it, trying to get inside of me. If I make the shower hot enough, it will kill them and I won't feel anything but the burning and stinging of the water, not the dull pain where Ethan was inside me, not the sickness, not the fragments of feelings like hiccups in my brain.

"Is he your boyfriend?" Mom calls from the living room.

"I guess so," I say.

"He seems nice," she says. "I bet your father would like to meet him."

"I'm going to take a shower," I say, and do not wait for her response.

I lock the door to the bathroom and turn on the water as hot as it will go. I take off my clothes, get in and feel the water like knives slicing through me. I close my eyes and clench my teeth and focus on the pain, welcome it, let it become part of me. I hold on to the wall as my back is pelted with water, burning through my skin and getting inside me, burning my veins and my muscles and fat and bones and thoughts and memories, burning me until I am nothing, until I am clean. I do not listen to the voice in my head screaming at me to get out.

There are voices you can silence.

(NINE)

It's a strange kind of quiet under a freeway overpass on a rainy day. You can hear the cars above you, muted by layers of concrete. You can hear the rain pounding on asphalt, on the metal of abandoned cars, on the wood of abandoned buildings. You can hear the boys on skateboards, their crunchy rolling back and forth, the wood hitting concrete, the scraping. You can hear the boys when they fall, their soft bodies hitting the ground, the skateboards flying, crashing, the shits, the fucks, the goddammits. You can hear all these things, but they're somehow small, like you're only hearing their shadows. You're aware of everything but none of it matters. You can see the boys' mouths move but all you can hear is static. The loudest thing is your teeth and forth. They occasionally jump or slide on a curb or a rail, something concrete or metal. It is only interesting when someone falls down. Ethan sees us watching, turns and heads toward us fast. We scream like we're supposed to and he stops just before he runs into us. He puts his arm around me and starts kissing. I can taste the stale cigarette smoke on his tongue. I can smell his sweat. I can feel his wet armpits resting on the shoulders of my brand-new coat.

"How do I look, baby?" he says. He's breathing hard and steam is rising off his body. He's posing for us, puffing his chest out.

"Good," I say. "You look really good."

"Cool," he says, and he skates off to join the other boys going back and forth.

This is the routine, except Alex is usually sitting with us and not kissing the fat guy with scabies. Usually, we are faking how impressed we are. But today, I turn to Sarah and roll my eyes. I make her giggle. I can do it because Alex is busy getting her face sucked off. I can do it because she's not watching.

"This is so stupid," says Sarah. "Why are we sitting here freezing to death?"

The guys are taking a break from skating now. They are tagging their names on the concrete pillars with spray paint.

"They're like dogs pissing on poles to mark their territory,"

I say. Ethan has already claimed most of the poles. Red and blue and green and black, *Aleph* all over.

"I have the alpha dog," I say.

"What does that make you?" Sarah says. She's swinging her feet like a little girl, drowning in the giant sweatshirt.

I look at her very seriously. "His bitch," I say. She laughs timidly and I laugh back. She laughs again and so do I, and then we are both laughing as hard as we can. We are laughing so hard we forget it's cold, we forget the rain, we forget Alex and Ethan and everyone else. There are just our faces and everything out of focus behind them. There are just our voices drowning everything out.

Sarah is trying to catch her breath. "That's a double entendre," I tell her. She screws up her face, which makes me laugh again.

"Why are you friends with us?" she asks, finally breathing.

"What?" I am starting to feel normal again. I smoke some more.

"You're too smart to be friends with us. You should be hanging out with those kids in your class."

"I hate those kids in my class. They're all boring assholes," I tell her, blowing smoke in her face.

"Why do you hang out with us?" she says.

"Because I like you."

I hand her the pipe and she inhales, holds her breath, exhales slowly. "You like me?" she says.

"Of course I like you."

"You like him?" she says, nodding toward Ethan, who is attempting a handstand. I shrug my shoulders.

"You like her?" she says, motioning toward Alex, who is under the sleeping-bag coat, kneeling in front of Wes with her face in his lap.

I look at Sarah and she meets my eyes and all of a sudden I feel like crying. I feel like telling her everything I have ever thought, every secret I've ever had, like that could somehow make all of this go away and we would not be freezing, we would not be watching the boys pee on things like dogs, we would not be breathing spray paint and exhaust fumes, we would not be sitting here pretending we are like these people, not like Alex with her face in someone's lap, not like the boys going back and forth, not like all these people going nowhere.

"You miss where you used to live," Sarah says as she reloads the pipe.

I shrug my shoulders again. I feel like I miss something, but it couldn't be that. I couldn't miss living in the middle of nowhere and having no friends. I couldn't miss being alone all the time.

"What were you like there?" she says.

"Different," I say. "Boring."

"How?" she asks, passing me the pipe. I inhale, feel the smoke softening the tightness in my throat and my chest.

"I wasn't very popular," I say, which is the closest thing to the truth I've ever told anyone. "And I was good. I never did anything. I didn't know anything about anything."

Sarah has a blank look on her face, and I'm afraid for a moment that I said too much. But after a while, she smiles and says, "That sounds nice."

"Yeah." I am thinking about the photos, the ones that are ashes, the people I'm not allowed to miss.

"It'd be nice to not know anything," Sarah says.

"Like if you could just go backward," I say.

"Forget everything."

"I bet you can make yourself forget," I say. "If you try really hard, you can make the memories disappear. You know how humans only use one-tenth of their brain? I bet if you just thought really hard you could control everything in your brain, even the subconscious stuff like in dreams." I realize I am talking like a stoned person. "Does that sound stupid?" I ask.

"No," she says. "I can do that."

"What?"

"Make the memories go away. Make it like it never happened."

Sarah's shivering again and I can't stand it. I can't stand

her so small and sad and freezing. I pull her hand out of the sweatshirt sleeve, squeeze it in mine, feel it tiny and bony and fragile and cold, feel it squeeze back.

"You're going to freeze to death," I tell her.

"I know," she says.

"Let's go home."

Her body tenses. "I don't want to," she says.

"Not to your house, to my house."

She almost whispers when she says, "Really?" like she's afraid I'm playing a joke on her, like she's afraid to get her hopes up.

"Yeah," I say. "I think my mom might actually cook tonight."

I stand up and Sarah stands with me. "Is she a good cook?" she asks.

"Not really," I say. We are walking now. "But it's better than microwave dinners."

"I'd be happy with microwave dinners," she says. We are almost gone. We are at the part where the overpass turns. We are almost out of sight.

"Hey, where you going?" Ethan yells just loud enough that we can't pretend we didn't hear him.

"Home!" I yell back. He starts skating over. We should have walked faster.

"I thought we were gonna go driving later," he says, which really means parking behind an abandoned building or at the end of a rural road so he can fuck me.

"We're not feeling too good," I say. "Probably the flu."

"Yeah," Sarah says. "Like we're going to throw up."

"Gross," Ethan says, his face twisted in disgust like the thought of me puking has forced him to reevaluate my attractiveness. I think about kissing him good-bye, but decide against it.

"Bye," I say, backing away.

"Bye," says Sarah. We are almost gone.

"Wait a minute," Ethan says. "Where are you going with my sweater?" He has this annoying way of calling sweatshirts sweaters, like he's too stupid to know the difference.

"Sarah forgot her coat," I tell him. "Let her borrow your sweatshirt and she'll bring it back tomorrow."

"No," he says. "Then I'll freeze."

"It's okay," Sarah says. "I don't need it." She lifts her hand to the zipper and I grab it, pull it back down.

"See, she doesn't need it," says Ethan.

"Yes she does."

"Tell her to give me my sweatshirt," he says, raising his voice.

"No," I say, and it is the loudest thing that has ever come

out of my mouth. There is something thick and hot and boiling up out of my stomach, into my chest, into my throat and filling my head, throbbing, red, heavy. Something is filling me up and the noise of it is so loud I cannot think. I am bursting. I would explode right now if something touched me.

Sarah and Ethan look at me funny, like they don't recognize me, and I realize I have done something very wrong, that whatever entered my body and moved my mouth must leave or something terrible will happen. I must make it go away. Just like Sarah, I can make things inside go away.

Leave, I tell the thing inside me. *Die,* I tell it, and just like that, everything is back to normal, like nothing happened. Then it is just skinny, quiet me again, numb and exhausted, with nothing inside but air.

"Okay," Ethan says. "Whatever." He has the same look on his face as when he imagined me puking.

"Thanks," says Sarah, not looking at him or me.

I have to kiss him now. I have to make him forget the voice that came out. I have to remind him that I am who he wants me to be, not someone who tells him "No." I pull him close. I bite his ear. I put my mouth on his. I put my hand on his crotch, squeeze gently, feel him hot and sweaty through baggy pants. When his breath gets heavy, it is safe to leave. I back away. I say, "Bye."

He looks at me, heavy-lidded, and says, "Are you sure you don't want to go driving?"

"Tomorrow," I say. I blow him a kiss, turn around, and start walking.

We walk in silence for a while, Sarah slightly behind me. When we get as far as we can go under the overpass, we stop.

"We didn't say good-bye," Sarah says, looking out at the sky.

"She was busy," I say.

"She was watching when we left," she says. "She didn't look happy."

I consider this and I know I should be nervous. But I am too tired to care. "I'd look unhappy too if I just had Wes's crusty dick in my mouth for the last half hour," I say, and Sarah smiles and we put our hoods over our heads. She grabs my hand and we step forward into the gray blanket of rain.

(TEN)

We run the last couple of blocks to my house and our shoes match the rhythm of each other's squishing. By the time we get home, we are drenched and shivering, our faces lined with streams of mascara, our hair matted and plastered to our heads. I can barely get the key in the door because my hands are frozen. I have never been so happy to be home in my life.

"Oh my," Mom says as we burst through the door.

"Hi, Mom," I say as I start peeling off my layers. "This is Sarah."

"Sarah, you're shaking," she says, and Sarah just stands there. I can hear her teeth chattering.

"You need to get those clothes off." Sarah flinches when

Mom puts her hand on the zipper, but she lets her pull the sweatshirt off. She has that look on her face like her brain has gone somewhere else.

"Let's go to my room," I say. She snaps out of it a little when I pull her arm.

"Nice meeting you," she says to my mom.

"You too," Mom says, like she doesn't quite know what to think of her. "You girls get into something warm and I'll put your clothes in the dryer." Something's gotten into her and she's trying to act like Supermom. These phases never last for long.

"Thank you," Sarah says, still half zombie.

I show Sarah to my room and get clean towels from the bathroom. When I get back, she's just standing there in the middle of my room like she's afraid of touching anything.

"It's warm in here," she says.

"Here." I throw her a towel and she doesn't catch it.

Normally I'd be shy, but I'm too cold to care if Sarah sees me naked. I start taking off my clothes without trying to hide anything. Sarah turns her back to me and starts slowly undressing, hunched over like she's trying to make herself as small as possible. I dry myself off, wrap the towel around me and start looking through my dresser for pajamas that aren't too embarrassing.

When I turn around, Sarah is facing the wall. Her shirt is off and I can see her pale, naked back with one long scar running down the middle, a half-inch-thick ridge of discolored skin, not a scar like I've ever had, not the kind from cuts and scrapes that disappear after a few months. This is the kind of scar that doesn't heal, that will last forever.

"Sarah," I whisper.

She wraps the towel around her and turns her head to look at me. She tries to look me in the eyes, but her stare falls into space, into something that won't look back at her. There is a look in her eyes that is intended for me, a kind of begging for me to say nothing more.

"Which ones do you want?" I finally say. I hold out the pajamas in my hands. There is red flannel, blue-and-green plaid, and half-hidden beneath them, fuzzy baby blue with pink sheep.

Sarah smiles, straightens a little, and takes a few small steps toward me.

"The sheep ones," she says. I hand them to her and we get dressed in silence.

Dinner is pot roast, and Mom is wearing an apron. Dad's seat is empty, as it is most nights, but Mom has set a plate and silverware and napkin there, like she's still hoping tonight will be different. Sarah is saying please and thank you for everything, like she has no idea how to eat dinner with people, but she's smiling like this is the best Friday night she's ever had. I wonder if she's ever sat down to dinner like this. I wonder if she's thinking things are always like this with other people, that moms cook pot roast, wear aprons, help you out of wet clothes and put them in the dryer.

Mom turns on the fireplace and the fake logs glow red. "Sarah," she says. "It's nice that you could join us for dinner."

"Thank you. I mean, yes, I'm glad, too," Sarah says, trying to cut her meat in pajama sleeves that are too long.

"I wish you would have your friends over more often," Mom says to me.

"I'll come," Sarah says, and we look at her. Her eyes grow wide and she nearly drops her fork.

"Well, you're welcome anytime," Mom says, and Sarah looks down at her plate like she's embarrassed for speaking, embarrassed for wanting anything.

"How was school today?" Mom says, and we both say, "Fine."

"Still getting A's?"

"Yes," I say.

"I'm proud of you," she says, but she doesn't mean it. Showing your kids you care was probably today's talk show topic.

Mom babbles about going to the grocery store, how she

had to drive around three times to find a parking spot. She talks about the good deal she got on the roast, how boxes of cereal were two for the price of one. I wonder if these are the kinds of things she talks about with my dad when they are alone in their bedroom. I don't blame him for staying at work all night.

Sarah listens like this is the most exciting news she's ever heard, like she's trying to take everything in, like she's trying to store it away so she can save it for later. I kick her leg under the table and she kicks me back.

"How did you girls meet?" my mom says. "Are you in Cassie's classes?"

"Um, no," Sarah says with her mouth full.

"She just moved here," I say. "She's Alex's half sister."

"Oh," Mom says. "The mysterious Alex, who Cassie's always going someplace with but who we've barely met." She looks at me like a caricature of a stern mom, like she's practicing, probably something else she learned on TV.

"Where did you move from?" she says, smiling to herself about her performance.

"Mukilteo," says Sarah, her smile suddenly gone.

"What made you move here?" Mom says, and Sarah looks down at her plate and pushes mushy carrots around with her fork.

"Her dad's in the military," I say. "He had to go overseas,

so she came to live with her mom until he gets back."

"How interesting," Mom says. "Where's he stationed?"

Sarah looks at me, pleading.

"Somewhere in the Middle East," I say. "Right, Sarah?"

She nods her head slowly.

"Oh, honey, you look so sad," Mom says. "You must miss him."

Sarah nods again, like a robot.

"We'll stop talking about it then," Mom says. Sarah is looking out the window like she wants to disappear.

"Can we be excused?" I say.

"You're already finished?" Mom says.

"Yes." I look at Sarah. She nods her head.

"There's ice cream," Mom says.

"Maybe later," I say.

I grab Sarah's arm to take her to my room, leaving Mom alone at the empty dinner table staring at the fake fireplace. "Thank you," Sarah says as I drag her away, and Mom looks up, her eyes full of weak gratitude.

"Sorry," I say when we get to my room.

"Your mom hates me," Sarah says.

"Why do you think that?"

"I don't know," she says. She's quiet for a moment. "She's nice. You have a nice mom."

"She's not always like that," I say. "She was on her best behavior tonight."

"But it's nice that you have her. It's nice she's like that sometimes."

"Yeah," I say, and I realize that my parents at their worst are probably better than anything Sarah's ever known.

Sarah sits on my bed and pats the blankets around her. "I like your room," she says. "It's better than my room." She sleeps in the room where Alex's father hung himself, in the room covered with graffiti and filled with broken things.

I open my closet and find the water bottle hidden behind the backpack Alex told me to get ready for Portland. All I've managed to pack are some clean underwear and socks and a toothbrush. All I've managed to steal is forty-three dollars.

I hand Sarah the water bottle full of clear liquor I've stolen from Mom's liquor cabinet, the rum, vodka, and gin she doesn't drink but keeps around in case of company we never have.

She takes a swig and flinches. "This is disgusting."

"But it works," I say, and I light some incense and open the window and we smoke a joint and share my pack of cigarettes until the liquor doesn't make us flinch.

We are lying on the bed playing a game I used to watch the girls on the island play, where you write things on each other's back with your fingers and the other person has to guess what you've written. I trace letters onto Sarah's back slowly, feeling for the ridges of her scar.

"Macaroni," Sarah says, laughing so hard she drops her cigarette between the bed and the wall, and we have to move the mattress to find the hole burning though the box spring.

"Oops," she says.

"My turn," I say.

We lie back down and Sarah just makes circles for a while, tracing a spiral into my back. It is the best feeling I have ever felt.

"O," I say. "A lot of O's."

"Hold on, I'm thinking."

After more O's, Sarah makes dots.

"Come on," I say.

After a while, she starts writing. *I-M-S-C-A-R-E-D.*

I feel the bed move as she rolls over to her other side. I turn over. *W-H-Y-?,* I spell.

We turn over again. *M-Y-F-A-T-H-E-R.*

I turn over but Sarah stays where she is. We are facing each other.

"He's going to find me," she says. "He's getting out of jail soon."

"But he can't," I say.

"A lawyer made a mistake. They're letting him out."

"They can't let him—"

"They can't do anything," she says without feeling, like it is something she has known for a long time.

"Sarah," I say.

"Do you want to know what he did to me?" she asks.

No.

"Yes," I say.

"The social workers told me. I don't really remember."

"Okay." I can smell her breath. I can smell alcohol and pot roast and cigarettes. It smells disgusting but I want to breathe it in. I want it inside me.

"They said he'd been raping me since I was little."

"Oh, God," I say. Her face is blank, like she's possessed, like someone's put this information in her and she's simply reporting it, a machine, with no feeling. The "I" and the "me" could be anybody.

"They said the doctors could tell from the scars."

"Stop."

"Scars can tell you how old a wound is."

"Stop."

"When I stopped going to school, they came and found me. They found me in the closet."

"Sarah." I put my hand over her mouth. I put my other

arm around her waist and pull her close to me, pull her so close that there's no air, no room for air, no room for hands, no room for anybody but us. And my hand is around the back of her neck and my mouth is on hers, saying, "Stop, please, stop." I am dizzy. I want to go to sleep.

"I'm sorry," she says.

"Don't be sorry," I breathe into her. I say it with everything inside me.

And she cries. She is silent, but I can feel her sobs shaking both of us. Her eyes are closed but there are tears seeping out and her fingers are tearing into my back. Her tiny, brittle nails are cutting though my pajamas, bruising my skin beneath.

"It's okay," I keep saying, even though I know it is not, even though I know I have no right to say it. I move my hand beneath her pajama shirt, rest it on the ridge of the scar across her spine. I feel her heart beating through her back, fragile and fast like a bird. I kiss her forehead and pull her close. I say, "Breathe," and she does, and I never want to move again.

We fall asleep like this, on top of the covers, drunk and stoned. I wake in the middle of the night and cover us with blankets. She has her eyes closed tighter than any eyes I've ever seen.

(ELEVEN)

"Where's Sarah?" I say.

Alex is walking fast and it's hard to keep up because her legs are twice as long as mine.

"I don't know," she says.

"Slow down."

"You hurry up," she says without even looking at me.

I am practically jogging to keep up with her. It is hard to jog in heels, especially when you have a hangover.

It's eight o'clock now and we just bought drugs from a guy in a car with tinted windows. I don't know what we got, how Alex got the hundred dollars she bought it with, or even where we're going, because Alex keeps pretending she doesn't hear me whenever I ask her anything,

or she gives me an answer that doesn't really answer anything at all.

"Sarah didn't want to come?" I ask her now.

"She wasn't invited," Alex says.

"Why not?"

"Why do you care so fucking much?" She stops walking
and turns around. Her nose is practically touching mine and I
can smell her sour breath and cheap perfume. "You're my best
friend, not hers," she says.

I don't say anything. I have made her angry.

"Right?" she says. She looks like she wants to kill me.

I say nothing. I can feel the tears welling up. I can feel
my chest and throat hot and tight like someone's standing
on me.

"Right?" she says again. She pushes my shoulder hard, and
I step back. "Say it," she says.

"I'm sorry," I say, and now I am really crying. The tears are
running down my face and smearing my makeup and there
are thick, dull nails hammering into my chest.

"Say it," she says again, her voice low, growling. She is
holding me by the shoulders, her big hands crushing me.

"You're my best friend," I whine through snot.

"Say it again." Her hands move to my throat. I can feel
her thumb on my vein, my pulse magnified by the pressure,

pounding in my skull. My breath is stopped. My voice is trapped under her hand and throbbing.

"You're my best friend," I cough, and it sounds like someone dying.

She lets go and I breathe and she lights a cigarette. She starts walking and I stumble after her, tasting her trail of smoke and perfume. I feel the skin around my neck with my hands, checking to make sure everything's intact. People walk by us, looking straight ahead or out at the water, anything to not catch my eye, anything to not acknowledge that they see me.

I feel my face and it is wet. I run my finger across the bottom of my eye and it is lined with black mascara, each one of my eyelashes imprinted with tiny brushstrokes. I look at my hands and they are smeared with foundation, like paint the same color as my skin, and it looks like I am melting, like the palms of my hands are turning into jelly, like they have given up on being solid.

Alex slows down so she is walking next to me. She hands me her cigarette. "Want the rest?" she says.

"Thanks," I say. I take a drag and it burns my throat, but I feel calmer.

"You look like shit," she says. She opens her purse, takes out her mirror, and hands it to me. "Here," she says.

"Thanks," I say again. I check my face and rub away the

tearstains. I apply more makeup as we walk. I make it look like nothing happened.

The party's in a part of town I've never been to. It's not even in Kirkland. It's past the arcade and over the hill that separates us from the big strip malls and the streets like highways, all the way over in Juanita in a run-down apartment building, next to the giant church the size of a stadium and the two-story neon sign that says JESUS, LIGHT OF THE WORLD. By the time we get there, the balls of my feet are numb and my ankles feel like they could crumble into a million pieces. All I want is a drink and a joint and a quiet corner to sit in until Alex decides it's time to go home.

Wes is standing outside drinking a forty. Alex throws her coat off in my direction, runs up to him, and throws her arms around his neck. They stick their tongues in each other's mouths while I stand at the curb, holding her jacket and watching people I don't know smoking cigarettes and drinking out of paper bags. They are all older and they are almost all black, and I feel younger and whiter than I ever have in my whole life.

It is only now that I notice that there's something different about Alex, that she has replaced her usual combat boots and fishnets for Adidas shell tops and baggy pants that hang so low you can see the top of her G-string. Instead of a ripped up T-shirt, she is wearing a red halter-top that barely clings to her tiny chest. Her hair is covered by a black bandanna, only showing her roots that are no longer green. I feel like an alien in my outfit, a baby, a white-trash alien. The guys leaning against the apartment building look at me with their droopy, stoned eyes, whispering things and making each other laugh.

"Cassie!" Alex yells, and I walk over, feeling the heat of eyes following me. The bass of rap music from inside the apartment makes the ground shake.

"Hey, girl," Wes says.

"Hey," I say.

"This party's tight, huh?"

"Yeah," I say. "Is Ethan here?" and all of a sudden I want nothing more than to be in the back of his car behind the reservoir, looking at the ceiling while I let him fuck me. It is not fun, but it is predictable and it is not here. It's a kind of script I have memorized. I know what to do when I'm with him.

"Nah," Wes says. "He went tagging with some dudes from Redmond High." I don't know why, but this seems like the saddest news I've ever heard.

"Let's go inside," Alex says, and I follow.

The apartment is small and cluttered and crowded with people. No one is dancing, but all the bodies seem to be moving, pulsing to the beat of the music. Forties are piled on a table, and Wes hands each of us one. Most everyone looks even older than high school. I hear a girl a few years older than us say, "Nah, dude, this is my *moms*," about a woman next to her who looks only a few years older than she is. This is just like a rap video, I think, except there are no expensive cars or champagne and everyone's a little less beautiful. I wonder if I am racist for thinking that. I keep hearing my dad's voice in my head saying, *Those fucking people*, when there is news about a gang shooting on TV, and I remember always being mad at him for it. I wonder if I'm a racist for being scared now.

Wes leads us to a door at the end of the hall, knocks three times, and opens it. It is cleaner and quieter inside and there are only a handful of people sitting on the bed and on the floor around a low glass coffee table. The music from the living room is still loud enough to hear, but the mellow R&B playing from a stereo in the corner drowns most of it out. The people sitting seem like they are closer to our ages. The girls look at us and smile and the guys say, "What's up?" and I hope we stay in here for the rest of the night.

A beautiful girl with big green eyes scoots over on the bed and I sit down. Wes and Alex sit on the floor and everyone introduces themselves. I am not so scared in this room with the party muted, but I still feel white.

"Did you get it?" Wes says to Alex.

"Of course I did," Alex says.

"That's my girl," Wes says as she dumps out a pile of white powder on the glass table. The boy named Jarvis takes out his school ID card and starts chopping it up. Wes and another guy do the same, and the rest of us sit and watch and listen to the *tap, tap, tap* of white powder becoming finer. Wes makes lines for all of us and they seem enormous, bigger than the ones I've seen in movies. I wonder if he knows what he's doing, if he's just guessing how much is the right amount, if anyone knows what's the right amount, if we're all going to overdose and die.

Jarvis rolls up a dollar bill, snorts a line, and doesn't die. He runs his finger across the glass and rubs his teeth. He closes his eyes and says, "Come on, baby." He passes the dollar bill and everyone takes their turn. By the time it gets to me, I imagine the bill covered with snot, but I do like everyone else did—put my finger on one nostril, put the dollar bill in the other, lean over, and breathe in as hard as I can.

It feels like little thin needles in my nose for two seconds, then nothing. Then a terrible taste in my throat like liquid chemicals dripping. I pull a cigarette out of Alex's purse, light it, take a drag, and wait for something to happen.

One of the guys says, "Uh-huh."

Another guy whoops like he's rooting for a sports team.

One of the girls has her eyes closed and is moaning softly like she's just eaten something delicious.

I hear Alex whisper into Wes's ear, "Cocaine makes me horny," and that's when it hits me, when the lights suddenly seem brighter and the bed is softer and everyone's more beautiful, and my body is lighter and stronger and sexier and more awake, and the hangover's gone and the music is beautiful and everything is perfect.

Wes and Alex are making out on the floor. Jarvis and another guy are talking about how one of their teachers at school is a child molester. The green-eyed girl is explaining to another how she made the blouse she's wearing.

"It's beautiful," I tell her.

"Thank you," she says, surprised at my voice, like she didn't even know I was there.

"How'd you get all those sequins on there?" I ask. It is a masterpiece. It is something that belongs in a museum.

"Oh, I had to hand-sew all that," she says. "It took forever."

"You're really talented," I say, and I love her.

"Thanks," she says, and she starts talking to the other girl again.

There is a buzzing inside me as I look around the room.

I am surrounded by beautiful people and white light, sparkling, the texture of cellophane. It cuts through the mattress, the floor, the table, Alex, Wes, and all these people I don't know. But it is soft. It is like dewdrops, like a ball of liquid mirrors, reflecting all the light on me. I am shining, squeaky clean, sparkling.

I gulp down my cheap, warm beer and it is the most wonderful thing I have ever tasted. I take a drag from my cigarette and feel the smoke lift me. I stand up, float out of the room, and enter the noise outside. The bass from the music changes my heartbeat. It grabs me and squeezes my throat, my chest, my heart, pulsing, like all my life is centered there.

The lights are out and everyone is dancing. I move my way into the crowd and feel the bodies moving against mine. I see a couple of the gangster girls from school and they nod at me and I nod at them. I dance like I've seen on TV. I dance with my eyes closed, my feet planted firmly on the ground, my hips pumping back and forth to the upbeat, downbeat. I am not dressed wrong and I am not an alien and I am not a white girl from an island. I am one speck in this crowd of pulsing bodies. I am part of this thing that is huge. I belong here. It would not be the same without me.

There is a body against mine that feels different from the others. It is not a temporary bump. It is not an elbow or a hip or a hand. It is a whole body. It is a man, older than junior high or even high school, at least a foot taller than I am. He is smiling. His head is bald and his teeth are white and his T-shirt is starched, hard and cold against my skin. His hands are around my waist. My hands are around his neck.

He says something into my ear.

"What?" I yell.

"I'm Anton," he says.

"Cassie," I say.

"What?"

"Cassie."

And we keep dancing. And he keeps lighting cigarettes and joints and putting them in my mouth, and the song changes, and the song changes again, and this one is slower and everyone's slower and I am slower and I start to notice how low the ceiling is and how everything smells like stale beer and cigarettes, and suddenly Anton is too close and too tall and too old and all I want is to go back into Jarvis's bedroom.

"Come with me," I tell Anton.

"What?"

"Come with me," I say again.

"What?"

I grab his hand and pull him after me. Little me is dragging this six-foot-tall man through a sea of sweating bodies and I can't go fast enough. I am pushing my way through. A girl says, "Bitch," and I don't care. All I want is to get to that door. All I want is that doorknob in my hand and the cool air inside. I want everything else muted.

I find the door and suddenly I can breathe. I push it open and everyone's still sitting where they were, except Jarvis is at his stereo trying to figure out what to play. It is too quiet. People aren't talking. The girl with green eyes is biting her fingernails. Alex is leaning on Wes and smoking a cigarette. No one seems to notice me enter.

"This is Anton," I say.

They look up and everyone seems happy all of a sudden.

"Anton, you came," one of the girls says, and he leans over and hugs her and kisses her on the cheek. One of the guys slaps him on the back and says, "Good to see you, man. We missed you."

"What's going on in here?" Anton says. He is staring at the pile of white powder on the table.

"You want some, man?" Jarvis says from the corner.

"Yeah," he says. "It's been a while."

"Me too," I say, and Anton laughs.

"Hold on, girl," he says.

Everyone's perked up and waiting for Anton to cut the lines. I realize that my nose is dripping and I wipe it with the back of my hand. He is not going fast enough. I drink the remains of the forty I left on the floor and he is still not done. I light a cigarette and finally it is my turn. He lets me go first. He is a gentleman.

The line he cut is not big enough. I pick up the card he left on the table and pull out more from the pile that has gotten much smaller.

"Take it slow, Cassie," Wes laughs.

"You just calm down, young man," I say, and everyone laughs like it's the funniest thing they've ever heard, and I snort the two lines I've made for myself and pass the dollar bill to Anton and savor the chemical sludge in the back of my throat.

"This white girl's funny," one of the guys says, and I realize that this is the best night of my entire life.

They are talking about something but I am not listening. I am noticing how soft my teeth feel as they rub against each other. I hear snippets of conversation, words floating through the air and meaning nothing: "out," "six days," "two years," "time," "parole," "trouble," "hole," "piece." None of it is as interesting as the tingling feeling in my hands or the fact that my feet don't hurt or that the smoke inside my lungs is making me weightless.

"Shit, man," someone says, and I look up. Everyone's eyes

are pointed toward me, and I look down to check if my skirt is up around my waist. I make sure there is no snot running down my face. I look around the room and realize that they're all looking at Anton. They are looking at the gun in Anton's lap.

I start laughing. This is not my life. It is a movie. I am high on cocaine and sitting next to a six-foot-tall black man who just got out of prison and has a gun in his lap. I hear my dad's voice narrating: *Those people, those people,* he keeps saying. *All they do is prove the stereotypes true.*

But no one else is laughing. I look around the room again, and things are not like I first saw them. Anton is turning the gun around in his hands with a broken look on his face, like he's only holding it because he has to. The guys are solemn, nodding their heads. The girls look worried, like little mothers. I am not laughing anymore. This is not a movie. This is a guy I just danced with who is willing to do something terrible because he thinks he has no choice.

All of a sudden, I'm sober. The light feeling in my chest has turned into concrete. The music sounds hostile. All the chemicals inside me are swirling around my empty stomach, making me dizzy. I get off the bed and crawl over to Alex.

"I don't feel good," I tell her.

"Lightweight," she says.

"I want to go home."

"Then go," she says.

"Will you come with me?" I ask her. There's no way I can find my way home alone.

"Hell no," she says. "The party's just getting good."

Everyone else is talking among themselves in low, serious tones. All I want is to be home in bed. I want everything to not be swirling and turning grotesque, everyone's face becoming sludge, melting. If I don't get up, I will pass out here on the floor and everyone will see. If I get up, I can hide. I can die in private.

I use Alex's shoulder to pull myself off the floor. "Get off," she says, pushing me away. I get up and stumble into the party, shove my way through the sweaty, smoking crowd. I get outside and it is freezing, but the cold makes the melting stop. It makes my body solid. It makes me see straight.

I start walking in the direction we came from and nothing looks familiar. All I see is concrete and abandoned parking lots. There is no life anywhere, not a bird or cat or even a tree. I keep walking and walking until I don't even know how to get back to the party. The spinning comes back and I puke behind a dumpster. I stay there for a while. I think about not leaving. I think about freezing to death behind this dumpster in a miniskirt and high heels. I wonder who would find me. I wonder if I would be dead or just barely alive, if I would end up in a hospital bed or a cemetery. I imagine my parents frantic, mourning me, my mother weeping, my father swearing silently to himself. I imagine them blaming themselves, and this thought makes me warmer.

But I am not dead. I am not even dying. I am cold and lost and miles away from home, but I can't be forgiven because I am not close enough to death. There is no excuse for me unless I'm dead.

There is a 7-Eleven across the street with a pay phone. The pay phone will call my house. My mom will answer the phone. She will pick me up. She will hate me, but only temporarily, and she will pick me up.

I make it across the street. I put a quarter in the hole. I call my phone number. I don't know what time it is, but I know it is late. I know everyone in the world is sleeping except people who are getting into trouble. I try not to notice the guy in the red truck sucking his teeth at me. The phone rings. Once. Twice. Three times. Someone answers.

"Hello?" It is my father.

"Dad?" I say, and I start crying. I don't want it to be him. I don't want him to be the one I have to explain to how stupid I am. I can deal with my mother because she has nothing to do but love me, but my father doesn't want me even when I'm good. He is going to be mad at me. He is going to yell. He is going to leave me here, stranded and freezing, with no one around but the man in the truck.

"Dad," I say again. I am not loud when I cry. He did not hear me cry. "Can you come pick me up?" I sound normal. I sound like nothing's wrong.

"Where are you?" he says.

"I don't know." My voice breaks. I sound like I am crying.

"Are you okay?" He does not sound mad. He does not sound like I've ever heard him.

"Yeah."

"Are you hurt?"

I am calming down. He is not going to leave me here. "No. I just need a ride."

"Where are you?"

"7-Eleven."

"By the arcade?"

"No. In Juanita."

"What's the address?"

"I don't know." The tears are coming back. *What if he can't find me?*

"Look at the building. Look for numbers on the building."

I look. They are there. A whole address is there, white paint on glass. "7644 Juanita Boulevard."

"Okay, I'm on my way," he says, and hangs up the phone.

I stand there for about fifteen minutes. The guy in the truck gets tired of me and drives away. Some guys I recognize from the party drive up and I hide behind the phone booth. I stay there until my dad comes, watching people drive up, walk in, walk out, drive away. I am invisible behind the phone booth. No one knows I'm here.

Dad drives up in his crappy old car and I don't move for a second. I think about hiding forever. But I am cold and it looks warm inside the car, so I leave the shadows behind the phone booth and walk toward the streetlamps and his head-lights. I am looking at the oil stains and gum littering the parking lot. I am counting the white lines that designate park-ing spaces. One. Two. Three. Four. The walk is a mile long. It is slow motion. I can feel him watching me, like the wind-shield is a movie screen, like this is a movie about the dumbest girl in the world.

I get in and sit down and his big winter coat is on the seat.

"I thought you'd be cold," he says.

I don't say anything as I wrap the coat around me. It smells strongly of something I don't recognize, and I realize that I don't really know what my father smells like, that I've never been this close to something that has been so close to him.

"Are you okay?" he says softly.

I nod my head. I still can't speak. He pulls the car out of the parking lot and we drive home on what might be the same route that Alex and I took to walk here. But everything looks different from the inside of a warm car. Everything looks different wrapped up in my father's coat, sitting in silence when he should be yelling at me.

"Do you want a milk shake?" he says, and I nod my head again. Even though I haven't had anything since a bowl of cereal this morning, eating is the last thing I want to do. But I could get a milk shake down. I could drink something cold and sweet.

We pull up to the late-night McDonald's drive-through. The lady shouts through the speaker to take our order and it makes me jump.

"What flavor do you want?" he says.

"Strawberry," I say. My voice sounds strange, smaller and higher than usual.

He orders the milk shake. I take it and turn toward the window as far as I can go so he cannot see me, so he cannot see the tears running down my face and into my mouth as I drink.

"Cassie," he says.

I don't move.

"Look at me," he says.

I turn my head so I am facing him. My eyes can't find a place to settle. I see his nose, his chin, his shoulder. Finally, I meet his eyes, but I look away before they see too much.

"Are you really okay?" he says.

I can see his eyes in the sound of his voice, and there are explosions inside me, giant gusts of warm, red wind rattling everything solid. I nod because it is the only thing I can do to keep from crying, to keep from telling him everything.

"Okay," he says, and I hold my breath until we get home.

Before he opens the door to our apartment, he says, "I'm not going to tell your mother about this."

All I can do is nod. I hand him his coat and suddenly feel cold. I go to my room and close the door, take off my shoes, and crawl into bed without changing my clothes. Even though I am covered with blankets, even though I am hugging my knees as hard as I can, I am shivering. I wonder what my father is thinking as he gets into bed with my mother, who will never know any of this. I wonder what it will be like in the morning, when we act like everything's normal, when we don't talk, like always.

(TWELVE)

It is the last day of school before winter break and I am behind the gym, sitting on concrete. Justin is sitting next to me and I am waiting for him to give me what I'm here for. I am letting his leg touch mine, letting his mildew-smelling coat touch my shoulder, my arm, my hand. I let him talk about Bill Gates and computers and microchips and macroeconomics and anything else that's in his ugly little brain. I imagine it is gray and slimy like the rest of him, smelling of mildew and old greasy food.

I have a theory that the closer I let him sit, the shorter this will take. But it has been four weeks now, four Tuesdays, and it always takes all lunch.

All I had to do was ask him if I could copy his homework, even though I didn't need to, even though I'm probably smarter than he is. But he doesn't know that. As long as I'm doing this, he'll never suspect that I'm smart at all.

He calls this "our dates." He said it too loud in class, "Do you remember our date at lunch?" and everyone looked at me like they were going to throw up, even Mr. Cobb. And all I could do was smile and say, "Yes," and remind him quietly that it's our secret and try not to burst into tears and run out of the room and out of the school and down to the lake and drown myself in the freezing, polluted water.

This is where Justin gives me his medicine and asks for nothing in return. Just time. Just ears. Just the blank look on my face that I have mastered. Ritalin makes him normal and it makes me invincible. I took four every day, then six, then eight, now I can't keep track and nobody has any idea. Alex and Sarah think he only gives me half his normal prescription, that we're all getting the same tiny amount to save up for the weekends. They don't know they're getting nothing compared to me. They don't know he gets his prescription filled four times more than he's supposed to and his mom doesn't notice and the pharmacist doesn't notice and his doctor doesn't notice and nobody notices because Justin is invisible.

Nobody notices that I don't sleep, that I sit up awake in my chair by the window and look out into shadows that are sometimes still, sometimes shifting, sometimes flat, sometimes textured and breathing. They don't know about the hole I drill into my arm with burning needles I keep in a little fake gold box Mom bought me for my thirteenth birthday. Even when I'm naked, Ethan doesn't notice the dime-size scar on my arm that never heals, the hole I keep opening and cutting and burning and scarring because it is the only thing to do at four in the morning when everything is quiet and dark and my heart is thumping fast and heavy in my chest.

This is too easy. It should not be this easy. I should not be able to slip a box of sleeping pills in my back pocket at the grocery store whenever I need to recharge. I should not be able to wake up and feel fine and do it all over again. I should be dying. My stomach should be falling out. My parents should be grounding me. I should be getting arrested. Someone should be trying to stop me.

I should not look forward to these meetings behind the gym, Justin's incessant chatter about things that don't matter, his awful, wet chewing on the lunch I can't eat. This should not be the calmest I feel all week, sitting on concrete behind the gym, watching the rain pounding on dumpsters, feeling so grateful that I'm not inside. There is no Alex, no Ethan, no James, no Wes, no gangster girls, no potheads, no tweekers, no skaters, no sluts. There is no giant glass wall dividing us from the normal kids who sit at their tables and eat their peanut butter and jelly sandwiches and plan slumber parties and play video games and fantasize about first kisses. It is just me and Justin and the rain and his sandwich and his pills and the weird things he says, things like "Your friends aren't nice to you," things like "You're not like them."

He is talking about microchips and he is excited and little bubbles of drool emerge from the sides of his mouth and hold on to his gray skin with surface tension or some other scientific principle he could explain to me. I am tempted to say, "Explain the scientific principle that makes your drool bubbles hold on to your skin," but I don't. But not because of the usual reasons I don't speak, not because I am concrete and my mouth is stuffed with glass. I don't speak because I enjoy my silence here. I enjoy listening to his endless ramblings, his words that do not matter. I enjoy that he wants nothing from me, just me sitting here, just my ears, just my silence. He asks for nothing because he is the boy who gets shoved into lockers. He is the boy who even the smart kids don't want.

I don't ask him about his drool bubbles. I don't ask him why his coat smells like mildew or why his glasses are held together with tape or why he sits alone at lunch every day except Tuesdays. Instead, I ask, "Is there anything else you want from me?" I do not think these words. They just come out, like a reflex, like I need to make up for the twisted gratitude that I feel when I'm with him. I don't realize what I've said until I notice that he's stopped talking about microchips, that he's looking at me in a funny way. He blushes, which makes his pimples seem extra greasy and extra erupting, and he wipes his mouth with the back of his hand and the drool bubbles are gone. He looks at me with his squinty eyes and leans over and whispers even though there's nobody around to hear, just me and him and the memory of drool bubbles, and pills in my pocket and erection in his.

"What do you mean?" he says, and his breath smells like beef jerky.

I say, "Anything." I am leaning closer, pressing my breasts against his shoulder. "Anything you want."

He thinks for a moment. His mouth opens slightly, then closes. Finally, he looks at me. Finally, he leans over and whispers, "I want to touch you." He sniffles. "I want to touch you down there."

"Okay," I say. This is easy. This is nothing.

He is shaking and he flinches at the sound of the zipper. He flinches when I grab his wrist and lead his hand down into the sexy underwear I only wear when I know I have a date with Ethan. He lets his hand lie there a while, not moving at all, and his eyes are closed and his nostrils flare with heavy,

to coming here. I was looking forward to meeting her. I was pathetic enough to think there is something important about meeting my stupid boyfriend's mother.

Ethan's dinner is ready. He pulls it out of the microwave and the smell of it makes me nauseous. I put the apple down. I watch him as he eats standing up.

"Let's go downstairs," he says, and I follow.

His room is in the basement, with two tiny windows near the ceiling caked with dirt. A giant TV sits on the floor connected to a video game system more advanced than the one my mom has. Posters of skateboarders in death-defying poses, and girls in swimsuits line the walls. Clothes are strewn across the floor and there is a faint smell of feet. The only furniture is a futon on the floor with an alarm clock beside it. Next to the alarm clock is a plastic margarita glass like they have at corny Mexican restaurants, with a huge cup and green palm trees on the stem. It is full of condoms.

"I have something to show you," he says, finishing the last of his dinner and throwing the plastic tray on the stairs. He has a look on his face like he's nervous and excited, like something important is about to happen.

He opens the door at the bottom of the stairs that leads into the garage. He turns on the lights. He points and I look at a large piece of plywood stained with spray paint.

"What do you think?" he says.

"About what?" I say.

"My mural," he says, still pointing. "It's what I'm going to do."

"What you're going to do, how?" I say.

"I'm going to start a business," he says, his face slightly fallen. "Painting murals."

I look at it again. Green, red, and purple blobs color a piece of cheap wood. There are some blobs in the middle that look like something close to letters. *P-E-A-C*, I make out. What must be the last *E* looks like a lopsided square.

"It's beautiful," I say.

"You really think so?" he says.

"Yeah," I say because I can't say anything else. "The colors really work well together."

"That's what I thought," he says.

I think about James the asshole and his Pink Floyd wall. I think it was not someone like Ethan who painted it.

I can hear the phone ringing in the other room. Ethan runs to get it and I can hear his voice answer, deeper than it really is, deep like how he talks to his friends at school, not like how he talks to me. I walk into his bedroom and his voice has changed back to his real voice. "Okay, Mom," he says, and hangs up.

He lies on the bed. He says, "Come here," and I do. I let

him undress me. I move my arms when it is time to take my shirt off. I move my hips and legs when it is time for my pants. I do this with the sleepy-lidded eyes I know he likes, even though I haven't taken a pill since lunchtime, even though I can see my purse across the room, holding what I need to feel good. I could get up now and go get it. I could tell him to stop and say I have to pee. But I don't. I know this will not take long. I know he will be dozy afterward and he will not question my need to go to the bathroom.

He fucks me and I lay there looking at this new ceiling that looks like every other ceiling I've seen—white, bumpy, blank, neutral. I rub my hands on his back so it seems like I'm paying attention. He finishes, falls on top of me with a sigh, rolls over next to me. I wait a few seconds and start to get up, sure that he's nodded off.

"Wait," he says, pulling me close to him.

"What?" I say.

He pauses for a moment. He looks at me with his droopy eyes. "Do you like it?" he says.

"Like what?" I say.

"Like sex," he says. "Do you like sex with me?"

"Of course I do, baby." I kiss him.

"But you just lie there," he says. "You don't even move. It seems like you don't like it."

"I do," I say. "I really like it."

"Do you . . . ?"

"What?" I am losing patience. There are pills in my purse waiting for me.

"You don't have an orgasm," he says.

What are you talking about? is what I want to say. *Girls don't have orgasms,* I want to say, but I already know I have no idea what I'm talking about. These are not things I know, not things I've thought about. They are things I've accepted by not thinking about them. I vaguely remember reading something about orgasms in the book Mom gave me, something about the best feeling in the world. But all I care about is getting out of here and getting to my bag and getting those pills in my throat and feeling the only best feeling in the world I know. I don't care about the feelings everyone says I'm supposed to feel, the things my body is supposed to want. My body is different. It does not work like everybody else's. It does what it can do, and that is all. It does what he wants, and that should be enough.

I kiss him and crawl out of the bed. I grab my purse and walk up the stairs, naked except for my socks.

"I love you," I call down to him.

"I love you, too," I hear, muted, as I close the bathroom door behind me.

. . .

"Shit," Ethan says as he pulls the car over to the side of the road. Rain makes a wet percussion on the windshield as he pounds the steering wheel with his fists, saying "shit" over and over again. I am leaning back in my seat with my feet on the dashboard, blowing smoke out of the tiny crack in the window. I am not concerned with his anger. The electric pulse of the Ritalin is making all of this okay.

"It's just a flat tire," I tell him. "Can't you just change it?" We are less than a mile from my apartment. I could get out and walk.

He doesn't say anything. He just sits there looking straight ahead into the black rain.

"Ethan? Hello?"

He turns his head a little toward me. "Yeah, I can change it," he says. "I'm just pissed because it's so fucking wet outside."

"I'll help," I say. I'm feeling generous.

"I don't need your help. I can change a fucking tire by myself." He gets out of the car and slams the door.

"Okay," I say to the dashboard. If he is mad at me, I have no idea why and I don't really care. I will just sit in the car while he changes the tire. I won't offer to help, even though my dad taught me last year when my mom forced him to spend time with me. I will watch Ethan's reflection in the mirror, smoke my cigarette, and not care about anything.

He opens the trunk and I can hear him rummaging around and muttering "shit" and "fuck" under his breath. If he says he doesn't need my help, then I won't help him, but it seems like he should have found the spare tire by now. I can feel the car rock as he pushes things around in the truck. I can hear things hit the ground.

Nothing happens for a while. I am waiting for the metal-on-metal sounds, the car lifting. I look in the side mirror and see Ethan sitting on the spare tire with the jack in his hands, getting rained on and looking like his dog just died. "This is fucking ridiculous," I say to the windshield, and I open the door.

"What's up?" I ask Ethan, already feeling the cold rain seeping into my skin. He doesn't say anything and I can't see his face. I reach over to pull the jack out of his hands but he won't let go. "Let me help you," I say, trying to sound caring or kind or sweet like I'm supposed to be, when really I want to get this over with so I can go home.

"No," he says, whining. "I should be able to do this." I have no idea what the big deal is. I have no idea why he thinks it's okay to let me see him pouting and pathetic like this when everyone else thinks he's the coolest guy in school.

"Why won't you let me help you?" I say, even though I'm wet and freezing and starting to feel like pushing him in the mud.

"'Cause you're my girlfriend. I'm the man. This is the kind of thing a father is supposed to teach a son," he says, his voice breaking a little at the end.

Oh, God, I am thinking. I am supposed to comfort him now. I am supposed to be understanding and loving because his father hasn't called or written in a year, because he didn't remember Ethan's birthday, because this man Ethan wants in his life doesn't want him and he should fucking get over it. I have a father and I don't want him. He can have mine. Or he can have Sarah's. Then he'll really know what he's missing. Then he'll realize he's better without one.

I pull on the jack again and this time he lets go.

"Don't tell anyone about this, okay?" he says.

"Of course not," I say.

"Promise?" he says, looking up at me with his pathetic, wet face.

"I promise," I say. I won't tell anyone what a loser he really is. I won't tell because if he goes down, so do I. I won't tell because I am nothing without the title of Ethan's Girlfriend. If he is nothing, I am something even worse.

I know what could happen if this got out, something as

stupid and small as the big stud on campus missing his daddy and not knowing how to change a flat tire. Alex could twist it into something that could destroy him, something that would spread around school like some kind of virus until it became uncontrollable, deadly. I've seen Alex do it before, when she convinced everyone that a girl in her gym class was a dyke and was watching girls undress. The gangster girls beat her up so bad that she had to go to the hospital. She never came back to school. Alex told me a few days later that she made the whole thing up. She laughed as she said it, with a crazed look on her face like she just got off the best roller coaster ever built.

I change the tire and Ethan watches, deflated and brooding. I'm the one getting covered in grease, my hands dirty and wet, my fingers red and stinging from the freezing rain, while he just sits there, useless. We get into the car and I wipe my hands with the used, crumpled napkins on the floor that are already sticky with fast-food grease, snot, semen. It is the night before Christmas Eve and this is how I'm celebrating.

Ethan starts the car and turns the heat on high. He takes my hands in his and starts rubbing. "You're freezing," he says.

"You're warm," I say, and he rubs his hands faster. "You have to get your blood pumping," he says, and I wonder where he's heard that before. People don't really say things like "you have to get your blood pumping" while rubbing your hands in a warm car in the rain. I look at him and he's staring at me, a timid smile on his face, his big, warm hands making a sandwich around mine.

"Cassie," he says.

"What?" I say.

"You're wonderful," he says. "I feel like I can tell you anything." He smiles a goofy smile and cups my hands in his, blows his warm breath into my fists, makes my hands relax. My arms, my shoulders, my chest, my throat, my jaw, every part of me turns into sponge. I am finally warm and maybe this isn't so bad, sitting here with Ethan, letting him think I'm wonderful, letting him think I love him.

He lifts his hand and touches my face, trails his fingers softly down my cheek. "You're beautiful," he says, and I look away. I catch a glimpse of myself in the side-view mirror and I feel something small break inside. My hair is plastered to my face, my eyes blackened by melting mascara, and suddenly the rain is too loud, too violent, and Ethan's face is too soft and his teeth are too crooked, and I need to be anyplace but here. The warmth is gone from my body and I am hard again, solid.

I look back at him, at his face still glowing and earnest, and I wish other people could see him like this, see him all sweet and sentimental. I wish they could see him this weak.

I could break my promise to him. I could tell. I could see what happens when someone big gets destroyed and turned into someone small. I could teach Ethan what it feels like to be destroyed. I could know how it feels to be the one who does the destroying.

(FOURTEEN)

I'm standing outside the fancy mini-mall where Kirkland has erected a big gaudy Christmas tree, where everyone has come to ooh and aah even though it's just a big dead tree strangled by Christmas lights. Here I am, the day before Christmas, watching all the people weighed down by last-minute shopping bags, the families on their way to see a cheesy holiday movie, the emaciated Santa with his crooked beard ringing a bell next to a donation bucket. I am standing still and everyone else is scurrying around me with flushed cheeks and Christmas sweaters, chasing sugar-drunk children and the sale signs in the shop windows.

It's bad enough in my house with Mom playing the same Frank Sinatra Christmas album over and over, Dad hiding in the bedroom to avoid all her cheap decorations, all her pretending that her collection of phony holiday crap makes things festive. Just being there, just seeing that fat plastic Santa glowing on the mantel, just smelling her cookies burning in the oven, makes me want to jump out the window.

I thought being outside would somehow be better, that walking around would force my heartbeats and breaths to follow some sort of order, that open air would make me feel lighter. But there's a place in my chest that still feels like lead, the *thump, thump, thump* threatening to tear through me.

I am waiting for Sarah. I am looking around, but all I see are white, smiling faces and multicolored scarves, all these people with something to look forward to, all of them with faith that tomorrow morning will bring something new. They will wake up and find their glittering boxes under their trees, full of all the things they had to have. They will open the boxes and their lives will be complete for that moment. Then there will be food and eggnog and a heavy night of sleep. Then New Year's Eve and empty promises, hangovers, and football. Then it will be back to work, back to school, back to everything exactly the same as it was before. The only difference will be the new date. The only difference will be the new sweaters, new jewelry, new scarves that they will stop wanting as soon as they get them.

But for now, time is paused. It is winter break and I don't have to go to school for a week. I should be able to breathe now. I should be excited like everybody else, thinking about all the fun things I'm going to do. But all I am is tired. I'm tired of Alex and Ethan and Justin. I'm tired of parents and teachers and drugs and sex, and I'm even tired of Sarah. But there is nothing I can do, nothing to make them go away. They are still here even though it is winter break. They will still be here when it's over. They will be here and so will I.

"Cassie." It is Sarah's voice. It is coming from somewhere behind me, but I pretend I don't hear it. She asked me to meet her here before I have to leave for my aunt's annual Christmas party, before she has to go back to an empty house, before she has to spend Christmas alone because Alex and her mother are with grandparents who don't consider Sarah a part of their family. I said yes because it would give me something to do, give me something to think about besides my dad's white-trash family and their tradition of sitting around in a circle of folding chairs pretending to want to talk to each other. I am here because the more I think about them, the more detail I see in their miserable faces, the more they become one face, the more I can't breathe, the heavier the lead in my chest becomes.

"Cassie," Sarah says. She touches my shoulder and I turn

around. "Merry Christmas," she says, her face lit up like she actually thinks the words mean something.

"I hate Christmas," I say.

"Me too," she says. I am imagining her home alone tonight, in that empty house full of garbage and suicide. "What should we do?" she says.

"I don't know," I say. "Let's get out of here." I start walking without waiting for a response. Sarah follows like she always does.

I head for the parking lot across the street. It is the only place I can see where there are no families or strollers or Santas or Christmas carols booming out of invisible speakers hidden in streetlamps. The parking lot is the only place where everything is still normal, the place everyone has left and forgotten, the only place not pretending to be something it's not. I am walking through rows of cars, zigzagging between red and blue and white and black metal. Sarah is following. She does not question the lack of direction.

I caress a red Porsche. It feels sticky under my hand. I tap the headlight with my finger and move on to the next car.

"Are you okay?" Sarah says.

"Yeah," I say. I touch the blue Subaru. It is cold.

"You're acting kind of weird," she says.

I should look back at her. I should tell her I haven't slept or eaten in two days. Instead, I reach into my purse and pull out a cigarette. I light it and blow the smoke at the car window, thinking maybe I am strong enough to make it pass through. Maybe my lungs have the power to blow through glass, to get inside something impermeable.

"Can I ask you something?" I say. The trees that surround the parking lot are skeletons. The sky is gray and will soon be black. There is no color anywhere.

"Yeah," she says. She is behind me. I am looking at the sky.

"Have you ever had an orgasm?" I say. I am thinking about clouds, about how they look soft but are really cold slivers of water. "I mean, do you, like, *like* sex?"

I turn around. Sarah is thinking. She is looking at the ground. She looks up and opens her mouth but waits before she speaks, and I can't tell if it's like she's embarrassed or like she's apologizing.

"I've never had sex," she says. "Not really. Not, like, with a boyfriend." She looks at the blue Subaru. She rubs her hand along the side. She says to the door, "I've never had a boy-friend."

I can see her reflection in the shiny paint, all distorted and blue and tragic. She is always tragic. She is always pale and weak and wounded and fragile and she is always following me around like a fucking puppy. I have a sudden urge to smash the door in where her face is reflected, to kick it as hard as I can, to find something hard and heavy and hit it until it is nothing.

"Do you want a boyfriend?" I ask her. I am seeing her in the backseat, on her back, her legs up and her eyes closed. I try the handle of the door. It is locked and I keep walking.

"I don't know," she says. "I don't think so."

We pass by a gray Honda Civic, a little nicer than Ethan's. It is locked.

"Do you think it's bad to not like sex?" I ask her.

She pauses, like she's thinking hard, like she's contemplating the car's paint job and tires and the meaning of life. Finally, she looks up at me. She cocks her head to the side and says, "I don't see how anyone could."

She is serious but I start laughing. She tries to smile and I can tell she doesn't want to, but I don't care because it's the funniest thing I ever heard. She is standing there with a weird grimace on her face like she's trying not to cry, and all I can see are movies projected onto the cars in the parking lot, all of them close-ups of a woman's face in the throes of movie passion, eyes closed, lips quivering, head back and moaning that movie-sex moan that's low and high at the same time, guttural and animal like some ferocious beast but also whiny and whimpering like a pathetic, starving kitten. This sound does not exist in nature. It is a special effect, made in some lab in Hollywood where they combine the sounds of predators and the sounds of prey, as if the two could coexist in the same body without destroying each other.

"It's open," she says.

"What?"

"The car," she says. She is pulling the handle of a white Audi. The door is ajar. The distant sound of a police siren cuts through the cold, empty air.

"We should probably get in," I say. It is the logical thing to do. It is winter. It is Christmas Eve and we have nowhere to go.

"Yes," she says.

"I'll drive," I say, and she walks around to the passenger side.

We get in the car and close the door and I suddenly realize how cold I am. I rub my hands together. I blow on them. I wait for our body heat to warm up the car. Sarah looks in the glove compartment, but there is nothing interesting—some napkins, a map of Seattle and the Eastside, an owner's manual. I put the seat belt on and it makes me feel better.

"Are you okay?" she says again.

"Why do you keep asking me that?" My hands are on the wheel. I am thinking of driving through snow. I am thinking of mountains. I am getting higher and higher and the snow is getting deeper and deeper. I turn left and I turn right. There are no cars on the road.

"You seem weird," she says. "Are you on something?"

I keep turning the wheel. It is a video game. If I crash, I have three more lives until my quarter runs out. If I run off the cliff, I will materialize good as new.

"Just the Ritalin," I say.

"But we did all that," she says.

"No we didn't," I say. I park the car. I turn to Sarah.

"What do you mean?" she says.

"Don't be mad at me." The cars are still reflecting the faces of women, but they are sleeping now, calm and satisfied after great movie sex.

"I won't."

"There's more," I say.

"More what?"

"More Ritalin. A lot more. Justin gives it to me and I don't give it to you." I turn the steering wheel as far to the right as it will go. It locks and I pull on it, but it won't move anymore.

"Oops," I say.

"Do you give it to Alex?" she says.

"No," I say. "And don't tell her."

"I won't."

The credits roll and it is the end of the movie. I lock the doors and it makes me feel warmer.

"Are you mad at me?" I say.

"No," she says, and I look at her. She has folded a napkin in half, then in half again, and now it is a thick little square that won't fold anymore. She holds it in her hand like she's thinking of keeping it, like she's proud of what she has created.

Then she opens up her palm and lets it slide onto the floor.

"You should be careful," she says, looking out the window at all the motionless cars, the blank screens.

"About what?" I say.

"I mean, just because it's a prescription doesn't mean it's safe. It's the same as speed, you know."

"You sound like a guidance counselor."

"Sorry," she says, and looks at me, still pathetic as always.

I smile. "Don't worry," I tell her. "I'm smart."

"I know."

We sit for a while looking out the window at all the cars stopped and waiting to be moved. A young family with a baby is fighting next to a truck. The wife is red-faced and crying as she holds the baby dressed like a little elf. For some reason, I suddenly feel like crying. That baby has no idea it's wearing a stupid pointy green hat. He has no idea his mother and father hate each other. He doesn't know there's nothing he can do about any of it.

"I have something for you," Sarah says.

"What?"

"A Christmas present," she says. I feel a dull thud in my chest. I have nothing for her.

"I didn't get anyone presents," I tell her. "I'm sorry. I didn't even get my mom something."

"It's okay," she says, smiling. "I didn't get anyone else presents, either," and that just makes me feel worse.

She looks through her purse, takes out a small red envelope and hands it to me. *To Cassie*, it says. *Love, Sarah*. I open it carefully and pull out a little cellophane packet with four hits of acid. I look at her.

"For us to do together," she says. "Just you and me." She is smiling, hopeful, like she just asked me to marry her.

"Let's do it now," I say.

"But you're leaving," she says. She looks at the clock on the dashboard. "You're leaving in thirty minutes."

"That's okay," I say. "Then I won't be bored at my stupid family dinner and you won't be bored when you're home alone tonight."

She opens her mouth like she's going to say something, then closes it. She looks down at my hand holding the cellophane, then up at me with her same old pathetic face. "Okay," she says, but I can tell she doesn't want to, and I don't care.

I pick up the two hits with my fingernails and stick them on my tongue. I hand the rest to her. She licks them out of the wrapper like someone's holding a gun to her head, and I think if she doesn't want to do it, she should just give the rest to me.

"Now you won't be so bored tonight," I tell her.

"Yeah," she says.

We sit there for a while not talking. I know it should be an hour before the acid kicks in, but I keep hoping that it will be sooner because my stomach's empty. But everything keeps feeling the same. The cars are still not moving and Sarah is still sitting there looking like someone died, like she wants me to feel sorry for her, but I won't. It is Christmas Eve and it is time to be festive and fuck her if she wants to ruin it.

"I'm going to go," I finally say.

"But it's not time yet," she says.

"I have to stop by the store for cigarettes," I tell her, even though I know she knows it won't take more than a minute.

"Okay," she says. I open the door, but she keeps sitting there looking at the dashboard.

"You should get out of the car," I say. "The people might come back."

"Yeah," she says, and we both get out.

(FIFTEEN)

The headlights of the oncoming cars are all blinking in rhythm to "Jingle Bell Rock." Mom is tapping her foot and humming along, Dad's wearing a tie that says "Ho, ho, ho" when you squeeze Santa's belly, and I'm chemically enhanced in the backseat, listening to the cars sing to me and, for the first time, I'm not completely dreading Christmas Eve with Dad's fucked-up family. I wish there was a way to feel like this forever, to not have to deal with the anxiety of coming down and running out, to not have to worry about the body needing to sleep or eat, to not have to worry about the money and ass-kissing and humiliation required to feel good again. I could become a scientist. I could invent the pill that would make me feel like this forever. I could make Justin invent the pill. I could marry him and pretend all sorts of things and he would make me the pill and it would be worth all the lies and slimy, smelly sex I would have to have with him.

Burien is not far, but I wish it were. I want to drive forever so I can stay curled up in this dark and soft little world where no one's watching me, listening to this Christmas music like bubbles bouncing in my head, feeling the cool glass against my forehead as I watch the city lights swoosh by. Red and white and green trail neon in front of me. There's the Space Needle with the Christmas tree on top. There's downtown and the office buildings and the dock and the ferryboat and the water reflecting wavy moonlight. There's Bainbridge Island, all wrapped up like a Christmas present with green, fuzzy, pine-needle wrapping paper. Somewhere on the island is my old house, square and full of some other family's Christmas, a big cardboard box at the end of a gravel driveway with decorations only the birds and deer and raccoons will see.

"White Christmas" comes on and my dad starts singing in a fake Sinatra voice. Mom laughs and puts her hand on his and he doesn't shake it off. They are holding hands and he's singing and the city lights stream by like silent confetti. I have found the perfect chemical balance and I could die right now, I'm so happy.

Here is Burien and here are the strip malls and the rusty trucks and the strip clubs and taverns. Here is the Wal-Mart and the gas station and the church. Here is a neighborhood like Ethan's turned upside down, the broken lawn mowers and mattresses and toys in the front yard, the yellow grass, the cars on blocks, the plastic reindeer and Nativity scenes, the red and white and green lights covering everything and trying to turn it into something beautiful. Here is my Aunt Lily's house, the glowing Santa lawn ornament, my family's ugly old cars lined up along the sidewalk.

And there is Uncle Charlie's shiny black BMW parked in the driveway like everybody knew to save that spot for him.

All of a sudden, the chemical balance shifts and I start feeling anxious again. I have not thought about Uncle Charlie. When I think about this family, I think about the assortment of El Caminos and other dumpy, dented American-made cars. I think about their fashion that is always a couple years behind. I don't think about him or his black BMW, his fancy suit, his cologne that smells like money. I don't think about how everyone tries so hard to pretend his presence is the most natural thing in the world, how the conversation always comes back to someone bragging about something, hoping Charlie's listening, hoping he's impressed. I never think about Charlie and the way he doesn't talk much.

I don't think about how he just sits there watching and grinning, silently judging us all.

We are getting out of the car and I can already smell his cologne. I am dizzy. The smell is clogging up my lungs. The black-green of the shadowed lawn is swirling around with Santa; fibrous dark plants and glowing red plastic are dancing, mixing, becoming something unnatural and sinister. Fanged Santa. Santa with bulging red eyes. Santa covered in black-green fur.

"Close the door and come on," someone says from somewhere behind me, and I do. I walk toward the light and leave the tornado behind me. It is now time to act normal.

The light sobers me up. Everyone is in focus. The aunts all bounce out of their seats and hug us because that's what they always do, smelling like a million cosmetics and hair sprays and baby powders. The uncles get up slowly to shake my dad's hand, their big bellies straining against this year's new Christmas sweaters. They say things to me and I say things back. I do not look them in the eye. I do not show them the giant black disks of my pupils. Uncle Charlie stays seated. I can see his hand holding a beer, his legs, his expensive shoes, but I do not look directly at him. I can feel his eyes burning into me. I can feel the grin on his face, the one that says, *You people are pathetic.*

"Charlie," my dad says.

"Bill," Charlie says. The sound of his deep voice makes me shiver, like it's an eruption inside my ribs, an explosion of cold air, spreading and freezing everything in its path.

"The kids are in Tracy's bedroom," someone says. "Drinks are in the laundry room," someone says. I make my exit without waiting for everyone's "How's school?" and "You look so grown up now" and "You must have to fight the boys off with a stick." I get out as fast as I can.

The laundry room is set up like a bar, a red tablecloth covering the washer and dryer. It feels safe in here, cool, quiet. I would stay in here all night with the lights off if I could, but I know people would keep coming in and out, opening the door and letting the light in, filling up the space with their fat, white bodies and stealing the air.

I fill a plastic cup with ice and rum and a little Coke. I take a sip and it is the best thing I have ever tasted. Warmth spreads through my entire body and all of a sudden I don't feel so much like hiding. All of a sudden, I feel like everything's going to be okay and it makes me laugh a little. I am laughing to myself in a giant closet because it's Christmas Eve and I'm on acid and speed and no one has any idea. I am laughing because I feel great even though two seconds ago I wanted to disappear. It's crazy how feelings can switch that fast, how something as stupid as the taste of something can change everything.

The adults are sitting in a circle in the living room like they do every year. Folding chairs fill up the spaces between the couch and love seat and armchair. TV trays hold bowls of nuts and candy. Mom heads toward me on her way to the bar and I slip into the bedroom before she has a chance to say anything.

I have three girl cousins, all born within three months of each other, all three years older than me, all living in the three neighboring towns of Burien, SeaTac, and Seahurst. They share the same friends. They go to one another's birthday parties. Here they are, sitting on the bed in the room with framed cat posters. They are sitting on the pastel, floral print comforter, surrounded by a hundred lace or satin or needlepoint pillows, surrounded by framed posters of cats with balls of yarn, cats sleeping, cats dressed up like sailors, cats in giant beer mugs. They are slightly different variations of the same person, with the same pale, greasy skin; the same mousy brown hair; the same plump, pear-shaped bodies.

"Oh my God," says Tracy, the leader only because she's the least homely. "Cassie?"

"Oh my God," says Kelly, the short one.

"Oh my God," says Becky, the zitty one.

"Hi," I say. I am number four, the alien.

"You look sooooo different," says Tracy.

"Yeah," says Kelly. "Like, way older. And, like, not ugly."

"When was the last time we saw you?" asks Becky.

"Easter," I say.

"Oh my God," says Becky. "You have changed sooooo much since then."

"Yeah," I say. *You haven't*, I want to say. "What are you guys doing?"

"Just talking," says Tracy, then she looks at the others like they're in on a secret and they all giggle. They look at me. They are waiting for me to ask what they're talking about. I won't do it. I take a big gulp of rum and feel warm and invincible. I sit down on the wicker chair facing the bed, like I am on trial and they are a panel of jurors.

"Want some rum?" I say, thrusting my plastic cup at them.

"Oh my God," says Kelly. "You drink?"

"Yeah, don't you?"

"Yeah, sometimes," says Tracy. "But, like, we're high schoolers."

"That's nice," I say. There is silence for a while as they stare at me. Then they turn back toward one another and just like that, I don't exist. I'm in another world on my wicker chair, an island, and their bed is some kind of country that hates foreigners.

"So what are you going to do?" Becky asks Tracy.

"I don't know," Tracy says.

"Do you love him?" asks Kelly.

"Of course I do," she says. "I just don't know if I'm ready."

I have walked in on an after-school special. The cats on the wall sigh with me. One of them rolls his eyes. The crystal unicorn on the bedside table is pointing his horn at them, threatening to use it. My cousins talk and talk in their hushed, important voices, and I am satisfied on my island of wicker with a view of all the cutesy crap piled throughout the room. I hear nothing they say. I am in a bubble of sound. I hear ocean, the inside of seashells, white noise.

"Cassie," someone says, piercing my bubble. I look up and everyone's standing. The door is open and they're all looking at me like I'm crazy. "Didn't you hear Aunt Lily?" says Kelly.

"What?"

"It's time for dinner," says Tracy. She rolls her eyes, they all start walking and I follow their chubby procession into the living room.

I take my place in the back of the line and watch everybody pile food onto their paper plates. I wonder what rich people eat at Christmas because it sure isn't mashed potatoes from a box or a giant slab of ham that has been pressed into an unnaturally round shape and covered with canned pineapple. I wonder what Charlie thinks about all this, if he's totally disgusted and lost his appetite, if he's forgotten the time before he was rich, when food like this was normal.

The only things I put on my plate are marshmallow salad and a dozen shiny, black, rolling olives. I sit on a folding chair and look at the pile of peach-colored goo, the chunks of canned mandarin oranges unrecognizable in their coating of marshmallow slime and shaved coconut. I take a bite and I am amazed at how good it tastes, how misleading the appearance is, how it looks like crap but tastes like heaven.

After all these years of holiday get-togethers, Mom still hasn't figured out that this family doesn't talk while they're eating. Everyone's supposed to sit and chew and listen to each other slurp, but Mom always babbles about something even though no one else says anything.

"Bill's going to get a promotion soon," she says. "Right, honey?" Dad doesn't acknowledge that he heard her.

Charlie kind of looks at her out of the corner of his eye.

"You're a stockbroker," she says, neither a question nor a statement. Charlie half nods as he butters his roll.

"Maybe you two should talk. I mean, Bill sells computers and you need them, right?"

"I think my company is doing all right with their computers," Uncle Charlie finally says. Everyone keeps their eyes on their plates, but I swear they are smirking.

There is silence for a while and Mom can't stand it. "That's a real nice car you have, Charlie," she says.

Charlie nods and the only sound is the scraping of plastic forks on cardboard and the ice of Mom's drink thudding dully against the side of her cup. It is a different sound than the clinking of her glasses at home. It is different, but it sounds just as sad.

I stick the olives on the tips of my fingers and eat them off one by one.

Everybody keeps eating and not talking and I am out of rum. I have eaten as much as I can, three spoonfuls of marshmallow salad and five olives. It is time to move, to get out of this room. I will get more rum. I will go for a walk. I will smoke a cigarette.

I put my plate in the garbage and take my cup to the laundry room. I re-create my drink from before. I take a sip and feel better. All I need to do is go back into the cat room and get my purse. Then I need to walk out the door. Then I am free. I can do this. This is easy.

But there is someone coming. I hear the padding of feet on carpet. I hear the laundry room door open. I hear it close. I smell the cologne that smells like money. I hear his voice behind me. "Cassie."

"What?" I say. I don't move.

"Why don't you turn around and say hi to me?"

I do what he says. I turn around and feel the walls close in. He is smiling. The door is closed and this room is too small.

"It was getting weird in there, huh?" he says.

"Yeah, I guess."

"I wanted to say hi to you properly, but I feel like you can't have a real conversation when they're all around." The smell of his cologne is filling up the room. I will suffocate if I don't get out soon. I start moving toward the door, but he is in my way and he is not moving.

"How have you been?" he says.

"Fine," I say. I can feel my lungs closing up.

"You look really great," he says. "You're a beautiful girl, Cassie. Do you know that?"

I don't say anything. I feel dizzy. My skin starts to itch.

"Because you should know how beautiful you are. A girl should always know how beautiful she is."

I can feel him looking at me even though I am looking at the floor. I am trying to focus on a space the size of a penny.

I am trying to keep it still while the rest of the floor swirls around it. If I can only keep that one space still, I will be okay.

"Can I have a hug?" Charlie says. I keep looking at the piece of floor. It is the only thing that is mine.

I feel his arms around me, my face pressed against his chest, his legs against my legs. He puts his hands on my back and pulls me against him.

"We should go skiing sometime," he says. "I could take you. Have you ever been skiing?" He is kissing the top of my head and rubbing my back and my eyes are open and all I can see is snow.

I need to move and I am moving and I am pushing him out of my way. My eyes are open, but all I can see is white. I feel my body squeeze between his soft body and the hard wall. I feel the doorknob and I feel my hand turning and pulling and I feel open space. There is white and there is more white. I feel the walls on both sides and the carpet under my feet and another door and another doorknob. I feel the button and I hear it lock. I feel the sink and counter and a drop off. Air. Smooth, cold porcelain and the poison coming out. My eyes watering and the poison coming out. My nose burning, my knees drilling into the linoleum, my hands on cool porcelain. The door locked and everything cool and everything okay. Everything out of me and I am empty. Safe.

Someone knocking. If I am quiet, no one will know I'm here.

"Cassie."

It is my mom's voice, dull and metallic like the inside of a tin can.

"Cassie, are you sick?"

My mom will not hurt me.

"Uncle Charlie said you're sick."

No one will hurt me if they think it's the flu, if it's something I ate. No one will hurt me if I did nothing wrong.

"Honey, let me in."

I open my eyes. There is white porcelain and brown slimy water and chunks of black. Everything cold and clear and in focus. I flush the toilet. I stand up and wash my mouth out with water. I rub some toothpaste on my teeth. "Cassie?" my mom says again, and I open the door.

"Oh, honey, you don't look too good."

"I think I have the flu," I say, trying not to speak in the direction of her nose.

"It's the season for that, for sure," one of my aunts says, and I look up and all the aunts and cousins are standing around the bathroom door, looking at me. Charlie's in the back with the palest face I've ever seen, his eyes wide, terrified. The cousins are huddled in a little pod, glaring.

"I'll get some water," another aunt says.

"Why don't you lie down in Tracy's room, hon," the other aunt says.

"Okay," I say, and my mom holds my arm as we walk out the door, all the women clucking like chickens behind us. I lie down and put my head on one of the hundred pillows.

"Not that one," Tracy yelps, and pulls it out from under my head. "Here," she says, and throws me the seat cushion from the wicker chair. I feel my body sink into the bed like I'm metal and it's pudding. I feel it swirling around me, a slow churn.

"If you need anything, we're right outside," Mom says, stroking my hair, and I have the sudden impression that everything would be okay forever if she would just keep doing that. Nothing could ever be wrong or scary again as long as she keeps moving her hand across my head. But she stops just as I become convinced of this, and I feel myself deflate, become light as ash, and the bed is suddenly not soft at all.

Tracy is the last one out. "Don't puke on anything," she says, and closes the door.

I lie there for a while, looking at the ceiling. I would do anything to sleep right now. I would do anything to be home in my own bed, five or six sleeping pills in my stomach. I would do anything to never have to wake up again.

There is a soft knock at the door. There is my name in Charlie's low voice. There is "I'm sorry." There is "Can I come in?" There is me getting up and locking the door, turning off the lights. There is me crawling into the corner between the bed and the wall, making myself as small and still as I can be. I am closing my eyes as hard as they will close. I am wrapping my arms around my legs and holding them tight against my body. There is a voice in my head drowning out Charlie's: *If you are still, no one can hurt you. If you play dead, there is nothing to kill.*

(SIXTEEN)

I would not wake up

if I didn't have to. I would not open my eyes and see the horizontal light that breaks through my blinds, would not see it bend and twist around the corners of my room like yellow cobwebs, like neon prison bars. I would not feel my head pounding, my throat dry, not taste my mouth with the acid fuzz of morning. I would not feel my stomach twisting in its chemical residue. I would not lie here looking at the white ceiling and wanting black again, wanting the heavy stillness of sleep, the flesh like lead, the solid absence of memory, the absence of sound and pictures and light and movement.

But there are instincts that I can't control, instincts that say "wake" and "live" without my permission. There is a robot inside who obeys, whose bladder says get up and go to the bathroom, who blinks at the sunlight and takes in breath. There is nothing I can do to stop it. I cannot lie here forever. I am not that strong.

The alarm clock says it's afternoon. The sound of Christmas carols and the smell of burnt coffee tells me Mom is out there waiting by the tree and pretending it's morning. There is nothing I can do to make it not Christmas.

I get up. I put on my bathrobe. I go to the bathroom. I pee. I brush my teeth. I gag and spit up toothpaste. I walk into the living room and there is Mom sitting on the couch in front of the Christmas tree she decorated herself, still in her pajamas. She isn't doing anything, not watching TV, not playing video games, not reading one of her magazines that shows how rich people live. She is just sitting, just staring blankly at the Christmas tree, just waiting for me.

She looks at me. "I tried waking you," she says. "Several times." She does not sound angry, just tired.

"I must be really sick," I say. "I didn't hear you."

"That's a shame," she says, looking back at the tree. "Being sick on Christmas."

"Yeah," I say, and I just stand there looking at the fake fire in the fireplace.

"I'll go get your dad," she says, and stands up, holding her back like an old person. Her slippers brush against the carpet as she walks, like she is merely sliding her feet, like she doesn't have the energy to pick them up off the ground.

I sit in the seat she emptied and it is still warm. I look at the tree and her careful decorating. I think about how bringing the tree home and making it beautiful was always something we did together, how she and my dad would carry it in and set it up while I foraged through the shoe boxes full of ornaments, choosing my favorites, the ones I would place. I remember how, after several adjustments, the tree would always still be a little bit crooked. It is perfectly straight this year. She paid extra to have the guys at the tree lot drive it over and set it up. We skipped the decorating ritual because Dad had to work late and I was doing something I don't remember. I came home in the middle of the night and there it was, lit up and straight and perfect, and I remember wishing I had not seen it.

There's the ornament I made in kindergarten, the beads on popsicle sticks in a pool of dried glue. This is always the one we'd put on last, right in the front, right in the middle, more important than the star on top.

"All right, let's open presents," Dad says as he enters the room. He's trying to smile, but he can't hide the fact that he'd rather be back in his room with the door closed, doing whatever it is that he does in there. Mom looks at him hopefully, but her face settles back into blank disappointment.

I take my place on the floor because it is always my job to be Santa. I hand them each a present that they bought each other, wanting to get this over with. I take one with *Cassie* written on it in my mom's messy handwriting, the kind of writing you'd expect from an artist or a doctor, not a housewife with a husband who hates her, not a mother with a daughter like me.

I open mine and it is a sweater I will never wear. "Thank you," I say to no one in particular.

"I saw it and knew the green would look great with your eyes," Mom says.

I take my bathrobe off and put the sweater on. It is itchy and too big. Dad gets a wallet identical to the one he gets every year. Mom gets slippers identical to the ones she's wearing now.

More presents and more crap no one wants. I get a cheap bracelet with hanging charms of roller skates, lips, a heart, and the word *sassy* in cursive. Mom gets a bathrobe and scented candles. Dad gets a tie and a set of white handkerchiefs. I get white cotton underwear and white cotton socks.

"That's it," Mom says, and glances under the tree. They both look at me.

"I didn't have time to make anything," I blurt out. "I've been so busy with school and everything, and I didn't really realize it was Christmas and—"

"It's okay," Dad says.

"It's enough that we can all be together," Mom says, another talk show sound bite.

I look out the window and the sky is gray. All the trees look wet and weighed down.

"Are we going to have pancakes?" I say. Mom always makes pancakes on Christmas morning.

"We already ate, Cassie," my dad says. "It's almost two."

"I can make some," Mom says. "We can have pancakes for lunch."

My stomach hurts and everyone is quiet.

"Well, I'm off," Dad finally says. "I have work to do."

"On Christmas, Bill?" Mom says.

He gives her one of his looks that says *I can't believe I married you.*

"Fine," Mom says, looking at her lap.

He stands up and kisses her on the top of her head, kisses me on the top of my head. I smell the smell from his coat the night he picked me up in Juanita, warm and spicy, and then it's gone. Then he's walking away and closing the door to their bedroom and the smell and my father are gone.

"Hungry?" Mom says, and I nod my head.

She walks to the kitchen and I stay sitting on the floor surrounded by wrapping paper. The Christmas carol CD is over and the only sound is Mom opening cupboards and paper crunching as I collect it all into a pile.

"How many do you want?" she calls from the kitchen.

"A million," I say, even though now the pancakes just seem sad.

"Okay," she says, and I walk to the kitchen to get a trash bag.

"We should start recycling," I tell her, just to say something.

"You're right," she says as she measures Bisquick into a bowl. I go back into the living room and put all the garbage into the trash bag. I put the bag by the front door. It will not be recycled. It will be put in the dumpster with everyone else's Christmas trash.

I sit on the couch and smell pancakes cooking. My feet are freezing so I slip them into Mom's old slippers. She's wearing her new ones now.

"Can I have your old slippers?" I say.

"Sure," she says.

They are warm and soft on my feet. I can feel where her toes spent a year carving into the fabric. They fit perfectly.

I sit there for a while looking at the tree. Something about it is not right. It is too perfect, too organized. The ornaments are all equally spaced, as if Mom used a ruler to decide where to hang them. I kneel by the tree and take off my Popsicle stick/bead/glue monstrosity. I find my favorite ornament in the back of the tree, on the bottom, the porcelain Mr. and Mrs. Santa in their red-and-white outfits, eyes closed, lips pursed, leaning toward each other for a kiss. I place my ornament next to them, destroying the symmetry Mom spent a lonely night creating. But in secret, in the back, on the bottom.

Mom brings in a plate of pancakes and a bottle of syrup. She has made a drink for herself even though it is still afternoon.

"Do you want to watch *It's a Wonderful Life*?" she says, her ice cubes clinking.

"Yes," I say. There is nothing I want to do more than eat pancakes and watch the movie we always watch at Christmas.

The DVD is already sitting on the coffee table, as if she put it there, waiting for us to watch it. She gets up and puts it in the DVD player. The intro credits roll and I scarf down my food. I have never tasted anything so good in my entire life. Mom lights the candles my father bought her and they smell like Christmas. I consider going into my room to smoke some pot and a cigarette. But my room seems so far away, miles, states, countries, continents. I am exhausted. I lie down and rest my head on my mother's lap. I feel her tense and slowly relax. I try to remember the last time I did this. My mind is blank. All I can see is Jimmy Stewart in black and white. All I can feel is my mother's breath and warm skin through her bathrobe.

My stomach is full and I am warm and I am crying. Rivers are flowing out of my eyes and no one knows but me. Tears drop and absorb into Mom's bathrobe, making tiny black pools that will soon dry, leaving no trace that they were ever there.

(SEVENTEEN)

Alex called and said

get ready because we're leaving for Portland soon. She won't tell me when, just "soon." She's paranoid like that. She doesn't trust me with anything. She probably thinks I'll tell Sarah. She probably thinks Sarah will follow us. She doesn't want her to follow us. She wants it to be just me and her. Nobody else. Just me and her and her brother in Portland.

My backpack's in the closet with more than a hundred dollars that I've stolen, a few dollars a day over the last three months. There are five pairs of clean underwear and socks, one toothbrush, one tube of toothpaste, a bar of soap, a sweater, a pair of jeans and two shirts. That is all that will fit. I don't know what you're supposed to wear when you're thirteen and running away to Portland and counting on a teenage drug dealer in a gang against fat people to take care of you. I don't even know what it means to be in gang against fat people, if they have a uniform, a gang name, a special handshake.

I keep thinking about shows I've seen, the movies with the girl on the streets, all dressed up like a hooker, all hard and tough. Then you always find out she's actually really nice if you get to know her and she's got some awful secret she's running away from, something so bad that living on the streets makes more sense than staying at home. Her tragedy seems so glamorous, and she's so sexy with her mixture of tough and sweet. She's always smoking and drinking whiskey, snorting things up her nose or shooting things in her arm. But then someone gets to know her, a nice guy or a nice girl who doesn't want anything from her. Someone gets her to cry, to tell her secrets, and you find out she likes pie and kittens, or she has an old baby doll she hides in her backpack and sleeps with at night.

I keep trying to think of something like that to put in my backpack, something special, something that would get a close-up in the movie about me and show everyone how sweet I really am. But I don't have anything that's mine, not really mine, no pictures of people I love, no stuffed animals I've had since I was a kid. All that stuff is gone, or it never existed in the first place.

Alex said she's counting on me. She said it in the voice that says I have no choice. I said okay and hung up the phone. It is sitting there on the pillow next to me, between my head and the white, cracked wall. I talked to her in the dark, the weak blue-gray of cloudy dusk casting soft shadows on my body. The light is almost gone now. I am almost black, invisible. There is only a warm sliver of orange creeping under my door, but it does not reach across the room to me.

It is the day after Christmas and school does not start for another week. I could stay in my room until then. I could fake mono and have my mother bring me food. I could flush the Ritalin and weed down the toilet. I could read and sleep and fatten up. I could return to school after Christmas break a different person. No one would recognize me. The kids in my class would say "Who's that?" and I would be someone new, someone good, someone to be nice to.

But changing is not that easy. Not after people know you as one thing and want to keep knowing you that way. Even if I showed up to school in pigtails and sweatpants, I would still be Ethan's girlfriend. I would still be Alex's best friend. I would still be that kind of girl. People don't just let you change identities, not unless there's something in it for them.

What I'm supposed to do now is smoke pot and eat sleeping pills and sleep tonight without dreams. I am supposed to wake up, do the rest of the Ritalin, then panic in a few hours when it starts to wear off. I will call Justin even though I already know he's gone for the holidays because no one's picked up the phone at his house in days. I will call Alex because she can get anything and I don't know the people she knows and I'm afraid to go to the arcade by myself. We will get fucked up and she will be my best friend and if I'm devoted enough she might let Sarah hang out with us as long as we don't pay too much attention to each other. Sarah will be quiet and spacey and her eyes will have nothing in them.

We will go to parties full of people I don't know. We will go to Ethan's house and watch the boys play video games. We will drive to the park and snort coke, and Alex will give Wes head in the front seat while Ethan fucks me in the back, and I will go to class and smell Justin all day long sitting next to me, feel his knotty finger inside me, and I will think of letting him do it again if it means I don't have to think or feel anything.

I could do all of these things or I can just stay still. I can lie here in my bed, not moving, not thinking. I can make the world stop. I cannot change it, but I can make it stop.

I am lying in the dark in my small musty room and all I want is neon, fluorescent light, so bright it drowns everything out, so bright that the darkness sizzles away into tiny particles smaller than atoms, pushed into the corners of my vision, waiting for the light to give up and die out, waiting for the moment it will come back and take over again.

"I miss you," Ethan says, his voice flattened by phone lines. "When can I see you?"

"Not yet," I say. It is six days until school starts. "I still have a fever. I'm still throwing up all the time." I cough to make it sound believable.

"I'm dying," he says.

"Sorry," I say, but I'm not.

"You know, you could convert," he says.

"What?"

"You could become Jewish. You could convert and we could get married and move to Israel. We could live in a yurt and raise goats."

"Uh-huh," I say. I do not ask him what a yurt is.

There is silence again. Sometimes when we are on the phone, no one talks for several minutes. The only sound is us sucking on cigarettes and blowing out smoke, occasionally coughing to remind the other that we're still there. I usually paint my toenails or do homework at times like this. All I can do right now is stare at the wall.

"I miss you," he finally says.

"I miss you, too," I say, but the thought of him touching me makes my skin crawl. The thought of anyone touching me makes me want to throw up.

"I hope you feel better," he says.

"Thank you."

"Take vitamin C," he says.

"Okay."

He starts to say, "I love you," but I hang up before he finishes.

The days are creeping closer to Monday. I thought lying in bed would slow them. I thought darkness and stillness and looking at ceilings would make them stop. But ceilings are not static. They change with the sun. Shadows rotate around stucco bumps as light moves east. The tiny mountains of paint are a wasteland with seasons. The hills of cheap texture record a countdown.

The phone rings. The phone is always ringing. My arm reaches toward the nightstand out of habit. My finger presses the button. My voice croaks, "Hello?"

"Are you okay?" Sarah says.

"Yeah," I say. It is five days until school starts. "How are you?"

I can smell lasagna cooking and my stomach growls. I have

eaten more in the past couple of days than I have eaten all month. People with the flu aren't supposed to want to eat, but I don't care. Mom says I do everything backward.

Sarah doesn't say anything. I wonder if she's zoned out. I wonder if she even remembers she's holding a phone to her ear. Any second now, I will hear it drop to the ground.

"He's been writing me letters," she says quickly, her voice a burst of distorted sound so loud I have to pull the phone away from my ear.

"Like what?" I say. It is just now that I realize my bed is starting to feel sticky. I wiggle my toes and feel something that must be a sweat-drenched dust bunny.

"He says he knows where I am. He says he's going to come and get me."

I lift my hand to my face and rub my eyes. I feel the greasy bumps on my unwashed forehead.

"He's not going to find you, Sarah," I say, too much exasperation in my voice. "There's a restraining order, right?" I don't really know what that is, but the lawyer shows on TV always talk about it like it's a big deal.

"But he knows where Lenora's house is." Her voice is sharp and quick and panicked. I've never heard her like this. Even that night, when she told me what he did to her, she did not sound like this.

"Sarah," I say. I am smelling lasagna. I am wanting to smoke a bowl and eat lasagna and drink orange soda. I squirm around in my sticky sheets and feel them make a noose around my body. Neither of us speaks. I hear Mom banging plates and I don't know if I'll have time to smoke pot before dinner.

"Hello?" I say.

"I'm sorry," she says.

"Don't be sorry."

"I'm going to go find something to eat," she says. Then a click. Then a dial tone in my ear.

I put the phone down. I try not to feel the new tightness in my chest. I smoke some pot to get the silence back, to make her go away.

"Where have you been?" Alex says. It is three days until school starts. It is three days until the world comes back and I have to be in it. It is New Year's Eve and I'm still in bed in my pajamas.

"I have the flu," I tell her. I do not tell her that I've been avoiding her calls, that I've been lying in bed smoking pot since Christmas. I do not tell her that I never want to leave the house, that I plan on pretending I have the flu for the rest of my life if it means never having to get out of my pajamas or put on makeup or talk to anyone ever again.

"Great fucking timing," she says, and hangs up the phone. No "Happy New Year." No "Get well soon."

I get out of bed and feel my body ache in the places that have not moved for hours. I open my closet and unpack the backpack designated for Portland. I put everything back in its organized drawer. I put the money in my sock drawer. I don't know what I will do with it. Maybe I will spend it on something. Maybe I will put it back in my mother's wallet, little by little, the same way I took it.

I go back to bed and the cocoon of pillows and blankets and sweat and dust. I fold myself into it. I will stay here forever. I will stay in my bed in my locked room where no one wants anything from me. I will let my sweat make glue and the air make a vacuum. There will be no up or down or backward or forward. There will be no here, no there, no island, no Portland. There will be nothing but me, immobile. There will be no direction but inward. I will go further and further inward until there is no place left to go.

(EIGHTEEN)

I wake to a buzz echoing
around in my skull, a long, tinny, mechanical swarm of noise
coming out of the wall and entering through my ear. I hear my
mom's footsteps in the hall, the unlocking of the front door, a
muffled "Hello." I have never heard this apartment's doorbell,
the sick architect's joke wired into the wall of my bedroom,
the speaker right where someone's head would be if they were
horizontal like I am.

I hear my mom's voice. I hear Sarah's. *Don't let her in*, I
think. I try to send Mom a telepathic message, but she doesn't
listen.

I hear Sarah's careful footsteps on the carpet, the timid
knock on my door. I consider not responding. Maybe she'll

think I'm sleeping and leave. Maybe she'll think I'm dead. I imagine her standing there for hours, staring at the door and not knowing what to do. But the image of her confusion makes me feel like an asshole.

"Come in," I finally say.

The door opens slowly and she's standing there, a black figure blocking the light from the hall.

"Don't get too close," I say. "You might catch what I have."

She closes the door and keeps standing there in the shadows. I can't see much, but I can tell her face is puffy.

"What's up?" I say, trying to sound cheerful. I have switched into make-Sarah-feel-better mode.

The dark outline of her body shrugs its shoulders.

"Sarah, I can't even see you."

She walks toward the bed like a jumpy cat sniffing a new person's hand, like she's waiting for the slightest movement to make her run away and hide. She sits on the edge of the bed, her body rigid, tensed like she's waiting for something to attack her. I don't say anything, just look at her haggard face and wonder how someone so young can look so old.

"I have to tell you something," she says, barely audible.

"What?"

"I did something bad."

"Who'd you kill?" I say, but she doesn't laugh or even smile. She squeezes her eyes shut like my voice hurt her.

"Sarah, what did you do?" I am losing my patience. I am sick of everything being so complicated with her. Why can't she just be normal?

"I told Alex about the Ritalin," she finally says.

"What about it?"

"That you were hiding it," she says. "That you were hiding it from her."

I should feel something now, but I don't. There is only the numbness I have developed and cultivated and turned into art. It starts with a *thud*, a soft bomb that hits my chest and spreads through my body, anchoring to my brain with black sponge. It is a numbness that allows me to wonder, "Should I be scared?" but it is only a thought, not a feeling, not real fear. It is a soft skeleton of fear. Porous, dissolving, lifeless.

"Why would you do that?" I say. Not angry, not anything.

"She made me." Sarah looks at me, her eyes pleading, pathetic. "She said she knew something was going on, that you had a secret you weren't telling her but she knew you told me."

"But she didn't actually know anything," I say. "You could have made something up. You could have told her to go fuck herself." The numbness should be dissolving now. Little sparks of anger and fear should be breaking through the black cloud and sizzling it away. But the most I feel are little tingles of something unspecific. I'm thinking that there are far worse secrets than this.

"Why would you tell her that?" I say. I am sitting up now. Somewhere inside I know this is something worthy of movement. My body makes me pay attention when all I want to do is go back to sleep. This is the most elevated I've been in hours and it's exhausting.

Sarah looks away and slowly lifts up the side of her shirt. I don't know what she's doing at first, but I am suddenly paying attention. The sight of her smooth skin makes me feel more awake than I have in days.

At first I see a shadow, a blue-black shadow on ribs and side and stomach. But the shadow becomes liquid, a lake of blood under the surface, pain turned into pigment. Then it is solid, bruised flesh stretched over porcelain bones.

"Jesus, Sarah," I say. She doesn't move.

"Did Alex do that?" I say. She still doesn't move, and for some reason I need to touch her. I lean over and put my hand on her ribs. She flinches, then slowly relaxes as I let my hand curl around the bend of her body. My fingers rest in the warm valleys between her ribs. I feel her distant little bird heartbeat. I can smell the shampoo in her still-wet hair.

"She said she wouldn't let us hang out anymore if I didn't tell," Sarah whispers.

"She can't do that," I say, but both of us know that's not true. Both of us know Alex can do whatever she wants.

"Are you mad at me?" she says.

"No."

"I'm not a good liar," she says, her eyes tearing up.

"Come here," I say. "Lie down." Sarah wipes her eyes with her fist like a little kid. She turns her back to me and lowers her body slowly, like every inch of movement hurts her. I put my arms around her and pull myself close. I absorb her warmth through every part of us that touches. She passes through my clothes and into my pores, into my skin and muscles and bones. She pushes all the numbness out until all I can feel is warm and good and full of Sarah.

"I wish I could stay here forever," she says, and I nod into the back of her neck. "My father could never find me here."

"He's not going to find you," I say for the millionth time, but right now it seems like it could be true. Right now nothing can hurt us.

Sarah turns around and faces me. "Promise?" she says.

"Yeah," I say, and all of a sudden I feel something. All of a sudden I am pulling her toward me and I am breathing in her breath and I am closing my eyes, and my nose feels her nose and my lips feel her lips. And she is soft and warm like Ethan and James could never be. And everything feels perfect for a minute. She is not beaten and haunted and I am not filthy and tired and afraid to go back to school. There is no school and there is no history. Alex is just a ghost, a bad dream. I would stay here forever, our arms holding on so tight we fuse together and become the same person, our arms holding on because we know as soon as we let go the nightmare comes back.

"Maybe you could stay here," I whisper into her mouth. "For a while."

"Really?" she says, her eyes darting open.

"Yeah, why not?"

She hugs me so tight it almost hurts. Her strength surprises me. "Thank you, thank you, thank you," she says.

"Is Alex home now?"

"No."

"Go and pack up your stuff, and I'll talk to my mom. I'll call you when it's okay to come over." I feel my heartbeat quickening. I feel the numbness burn away.

"What are you going to tell her?" Her eyes are big, like she knows the nightmare is close, pushing against the walls, threatening to break back in.

"I don't know." I imagine Sarah back at Alex's house packing her things, terrified of getting caught. I imagine her walking out the door of that crazy house and never going back. I imagine her eating dinner with us, my dad making jokes, my mom laughing. I imagine her in my bed every night just like this.

"I'll tell her Lenora's not feeding you," I say. I'm talking fast. My mouth can't keep up with my brain and my heartbeat.

"You wouldn't even be lying," Sarah says, and she laughs and all of a sudden she doesn't look so old. She looks like she should look, like a kid, not worn down and beaten.

"Yes," I say. "Okay." And I grab the sides of her face and kiss her. For the first time I see something in her eyes like a sparkle, like some kind of life burning inside her. "Let's go," I say, and she jumps from the bed and gives a silly wave as she runs out the door.

"Everything's going to be okay!" I yell after her, and somehow I think it could actually be true.

I explain to my mother that Sarah's being neglected. I say all the words the talk show ladies say, and Mom furrows her brows in concern like an audience member who knows the camera could catch her at any moment. "Of course she can stay here for a little while," Mom says, just like I knew she would. "That poor girl."

"She's really polite and everything," I say. "She totally won't be a burden."

"Should we call someone? Can we get ahold of her father? I'm sure the military has a way of getting ahold of people for emergencies."

"Not her dad," I say. "He's on a secret mission."

"Oh, dear," Mom says, wringing her hands. "We have to tell someone, don't we? Maybe I should talk to her mom."

"But she's crazy, Mom," I say. "Really crazy. That's who we're saving her from."

"Oh, dear," she says again.

"We'll figure it out later," I say.

"You're right," she says, and I can tell that the rusty machinery in her head is starting to work. "What Sarah needs right now is a safe place."

"Right."

She puts her hand on my shoulder and looks me in the eye. "You're a good person, Cassie," she says. My heart sinks and I feel like crying, like hugging her, like telling her everything. But all I do is say, "Thanks," and run to my room to call Sarah even though I know there's no way she could have made it home yet. I dial the number even though I know it's just going to keep ringing and ringing. I do it because I have to do something. I listen to the phone ring and at least it sounds like something happening.

But someone picks up. All of a sudden there's a hello and it's Alex. Alex who is not supposed to be home right now. Alex who can't know anything. I think about hanging up, but my thoughts do not travel to my hand fast enough. My hand is paralyzed, stone. I don't say anything. I just stand in the middle of my room holding the phone to my ear.

"Hello?" she says. "Goddammit, Cassie, is that you?"

"Hi," I say, and it sounds like something croaking.

"You fucking pissed me off," she says.

"I'm sorry."

"You can't fucking keep secrets from me."

"I'm sorry."

"You were fucking stealing from me."

"I'm sorry."

"Stop saying you're fucking sorry."

I don't say anything. The only sound is her angry breath blasting into the telephone, making me flinch every time she exhales. I look at the wall and it is flat and white. I look at the window and the shadowy outlines of trees. I look at the bed and the messed-up sheets and the place where Sarah just was, where she will return, where it felt for a moment like everything was going to be okay.

Then suddenly, Alex's breath sounds like nothing, just breath, just air, innocuous, harmless. I can smell it through the phone, foul and ugly. I can see her thin, chapped lips and the white hair above her mouth. I see her skinny, crooked nose; her blotchy, pale skin; her empty, beady eyes. I see her big ugly face and I want nothing to do with it. I am thinking, *How is it stealing to do drugs Justin gave me?* I am thinking, *I owe Alex nothing.* I am thinking, *I am not sorry for anything.*

Alex finally speaks: "We're leaving tomorrow."

"Leaving for where?" I say, even though I know.

"Portland, dummy. Get your shit ready. We're leaving from school. You didn't spend the money did you?"

"No." It's my money, my mom's money. Not Alex's.

"Are you ready?"

I try to think about what to say, the perfect thing that won't get me in trouble. I try to think about some magical way I can make everything okay, but nothing comes. My mind is blank, clean, spotless.

All I can say is, "No."

"What?"

"No."

"'No,' what? 'No,' like you're not ready? Jesus, Cassie."

I always thought the way she said "Jesus, Cassie," was like how my dad said it. But there's a difference: He says it like I let him down; she says it like she's going to kill me.

"'No,' like I'm not going," I say, and I'm surprised how

easily it slips out. I didn't have to think about it. I didn't have to plan it and worry about how it would sound. There it is, hanging somewhere in the phone line between us, somewhere stuck in electricity and waiting.

"What?" she says. I can see her face getting red. I can see her face turning into a pit bull's.

"I don't want to go anymore," I say. "I changed my mind."

"You can't fucking change your mind," she says, her voice getting low and hard, gravelly, growling.

There is silence. I am supposed to cower now. I am supposed to ask for forgiveness.

"Yes I can," I say, and I can hear her stop breathing.

"You're dead," she says, and hangs up the phone.

There's a dull thud in my chest at the sound of the crashing receiver. There's a sound in my ears like when you stand up too fast, like buzzing echoes from far away. Everything is still and hard and silent. This is the feeling of everything changing. This is the feeling in the place that is nowhere, empty, the beginning and ending of everything.

I need to get out of my room. I need to take a shower. I turn the water on hot and scrub off the days of sleep and cigarettes and pot smoke. I scrub off history and silence and secrets and drugs and sex. I scrub off Alex and Ethan and James and

Justin and Uncle Charlie. I am clean and nothing is the same. I put on new clothes. I sit on the couch and listen to Mom tell Dad what is happening. I watch him nod and grow quiet. I hear him say, "Yes." I hear him say, "The poor girl." I see him look at me, his always anger gone and replaced by something softer, sadder, and I feel myself love him.

I watch TV with my parents with the cordless telephone in my lap. I watch perfect families eat dinner to a symphony of laugh tracks, their problems monumental things like the kid's bad grades and the mom's PMS. At the commercial break, Mom tells me to call Sarah, and I do even though Alex picks up every time. I hang up as fast as I can and tell Mom the line's busy. I don't tell her about Alex screaming into the phone that she's going to kill me.

I try to watch TV, to put my face on one of the happy children. I try to be the popular one everyone loves, whose only problem is bad grades. But I keep picturing Sarah waiting next to her packed bags in the haunted bedroom, wondering why I haven't called yet. She should know why I can't call. She should know that Alex won't let me talk to her. She should know she can go to a pay phone, that she can come over as soon as she's ready. She should know that I am here waiting for her.

I keep checking to make sure the phone is charged, that

the ringer is on, that it hasn't been left off the hook. But Sarah does not call. It is eleven and the news is on and she hasn't called.

"Go to bed," Mom says. "You'll see Sarah at school tomorrow."

But I can't sleep. I've been sleeping for a week and all my sleep's used up. I try reading. I do next week's homework. I listen to the radio turned down low. I think about Sarah in her room, wide awake like me, waiting for tomorrow. I wonder if she's still excited, if she still believes what I said about everything being okay. Or is the nightmare seeping back in? Is she sitting in the haunted room and wondering if the two of us are enough?

I watch the room slowly fill up with daylight. I get dressed and go to school.

(NINETEEN)

I walk down the hill to the lake where Ethan picks me up every morning. I look at Seattle, dull and lifeless under the low gray sky, not green and sparkling like it always is in magazines and on TV. There's nothing beautiful about the concrete and metal towers of downtown, the wooden boxes flanking the hills, the stupid Space Needle like a giant cheap toy.

It's so windy the lake has waves. Water breaks over the rocks and sprays the sidewalk where I am standing. I don't move, just let my jeans turn dark with water, just let it run down my legs and make puddles in my shoes. I wish the lake was salt water. I wish the rocks were not smooth and round. I wish this was the ocean and there was nothing on the other side.

Ethan doesn't show up. I wait until my legs are drenched and my teeth are chattering and the first bell has probably already rung. I could go back home and have Mom drive me. I could jump into the water and swim to the locks that connect the lake to Puget Sound. I could emerge on the other side, in salt water, and I could swim back to the island, back to the house in the middle of the forest, back to where it was quiet and no one wanted anything to do with me.

But I start walking. It is three miles to school, but I start walking because moving makes me not have to think. I can focus on the sting in my lungs as I climb the hill, the muscles in my legs, my arms pumping back and forth, the wind, the wet denim sticking to my legs, the numbness in my fingertips. I feel the blood moving through my limbs, my breath going in and out, all the tiny cells speeding through the tunnels of my bloodstream. I don't have to think about why Ethan didn't pick me up. I don't have to think about Alex or Sarah or where I am going.

The halls are empty. Everyone's in classrooms pretending to learn and I'm in the hall dripping on the floor. It started raining four blocks ago and I ran the rest of the way here. But you can't outrun rain. You can't outrun something that's coming down on you instead of from behind. I'm panting, my shoes are squishing, and the bathroom mirror tells me I look like a homeless person. I crouch under the hand dryer until my hair is tangled and frizzy and my clothes are only damp and warm instead of cold and soaked. I put my hair in a ponytail and assess the damage. I would be passable if I were someone other than me, if I were someplace else where no one knew who I was. I did not put on makeup this morning. I am wearing a sweater and jeans. I am wearing my naked face that no one has seen since the first week of school.

I walk by Alex's class and duck under the window.

I walk by Sarah's class and she is not in her normal seat in the back corner. She could have changed seats. She could be somewhere that I can't see, somewhere on the other side of the room.

I walk by Ethan's class and I catch his eye, but he looks away. I stand there and keep looking, thinking he must be playing a game because usually he starts licking his lips or something vulgar, and then the teacher catches him and shoos me away. But he's looking at the book on his desk like he wants to kill it, burning holes into it with his eyes.

Something is very wrong.

When I walk into class, everyone turns around and looks at me like they do every time I'm late.

"An hour, Cassie?" says Mr. Cobb. "You might as well not bother." Someone laughs and it sounds sharper than usual.

I nod and mutter, "Sorry." Usually, everyone turns back around by now. They usually return to whatever they're doing as soon as Mr. Cobb is done humiliating me. But the girls keep looking, glaring harder than they ever have. The guys are laughing under their breath, catching each others' eyes, and smiling crooked smiles. I walk to my desk and someone coughs, "Slut."

I try to act like everything's normal. I take out my notebook and pen and pretend I'm paying attention to whatever Mr. Cobb says. But all I'm doing is trying to keep from screaming. All I'm doing is clenching my teeth to keep my eyes from turning into water, waves crashing against rocks, to keep from picking up my desk and throwing it out the window.

I stay in the classroom during break because I'm not ready for whatever's out there. I can hear all the normal students going to their next classes, all the gifted students standing in the hall outside the door, waiting to come back inside. They never stray too far, never venture into the rest of the school except when they have to for lunch or gym class.

It's only me and Justin left. I shuffle the papers on my desk, trying to look busy.

"Hey, Cassie," he says.

"What?"

"How was your vacation?"

"Fine." I don't tell him I called his house twenty times because I ran out of Ritalin.

"I went to my dad's house in Wenatchee."

"That's nice," I say. I don't even have the energy to be mean to him.

"Is it true what everyone's saying?"

"About what?"

"About you."

His face is worried, wrinkled. Everything is suddenly very quiet and I realize that I'm not breathing, that I didn't sleep last night and there are no drugs in my body to help me pretend I'm awake, no drugs to help me pretend I'm not terrified.

I look around the room to make sure no one's here. There's just Mr. Cobb at his desk grading papers. I lean over and whisper, "What are they saying?" It could be anything. It could be something stupid. It could be something worse.

He leans over and I can smell the musty stench of him. His lips quiver as he whispers, "Everyone's saying you had sex with the whole Redmond High football team." He pauses. "At the same time."

"What?" I blurt out, half laugh, half scream. "That's

fucking ridiculous." Mr. Cobb looks up from his desk and raises his eyebrows, so I quiet down. "Who's saying that?"

"I don't know. Everyone," Justin says. "Is it true?" He looks like he did that day next to the dumpster, all ugly and horny and hopeful.

"No, it's not true," I say. He looks disappointed. "Do people actually believe it?"

He shrugs his shoulders. "People will believe anything."

I don't move when the bell for lunch rings. I try to be invisible, but Mr. Cobb says, "You can't stay in the room during lunch, Cassie," and he doesn't even try to hide the smug look on his face.

The traffic in the hallway pushes me toward the lunchroom. I feel everyone's eyes on me, hear their satisfied whispers. I want to turn around, but I keep thinking of Sarah stranded in the middle of the cafeteria. I think about her waiting for me, more scared than I am, and I keep walking. I will get her and we will run out of this place. We will leave and never come back.

I stay close to the wall and look around the lunchroom for Sarah. There is Alex holding court at the cool table where I was once crowned Cassie the Beautiful Seventh Grader, like that meant something, like the stupid title could transform me. There is Wes with his hand on Alex's skinny ass. There's James making out with his slut, and there's Ethan pouring whiskey into his Coke, looking sad in public and not caring who sees. There are the gifted kids and the jocks and the nerds. There's everyone at their designated tables, their little islands of identity they cling to like their lives depend on it. In the middle is everyone else, everyone who is too boring for anyone to bother defining. They are not gifted, not beautiful, not rich, not tough, not repulsive. They are not anything controversial, not loved, not hated, not feared. I want to see Sarah there. I want to see her sitting at one of those tables, looking like everyone else, talking about a stupid movie she just saw. I want to see myself sitting next to her, planning a sleepover or a trip to the mall.

But Sarah is not there. She is not at the cool table that tolerated her because she was my friend. She is not in line buying food with money she doesn't have. She is not anywhere.

Someone yells my name from across the lunchroom. The room falls silent and everyone turns their heads to look at me. All the extras are perfectly synchronized. The spotlight is shining. This is my new role in the new movie. This is my close-up. This is when my face turns white and I forget my lines.

"Hey, Cassie!" yells one of the slut girls who has taken my old seat next to Alex. "Why aren't you sitting with us? Is something wrong? Do you want to talk about it?" Everyone laughs except Ethan, who is pretending he doesn't see me, who is drinking whiskey out of the bottle now, not even bothering to disguise it in his Coke. Alex is staring at me with that crazy smile on her face, and her eyes don't look human. They are the eyes of someone who could skin a cat with her brother, someone who could beat up her sister, someone who could destroy her best friend for doing nothing but deciding something for herself.

I turn around and search for the door that goes outside, the door that will take me behind the gym, next to the dumpsters, where I will find Justin and the pills that will make all of this go away. I hear the lunchroom laughing. I don't have the strength to stop the tears bursting out of my eyes. I run to the dumpster and I've never been so happy to see Justin in my life. He's sitting on the cold concrete, cross-legged, eating a limp sandwich, looking out at the dreary field.

I stand in front of him in my still-damp clothes, my hair a mess, tears running down my face.

"You're having a bad day, huh?" he says.

I nod and a little whimper comes out of my mouth that sounds like the most pathetic noise ever made.

"That's too bad," he says, and takes a bite of his sandwich.

"Justin," I manage to say. "Do you have any of those pills?"

He stops chewing and considers me for a moment. A look crosses his face like none I've ever seen on him, a look I didn't think was possible. Justin pities me.

He swallows. "My mom started monitoring," he says. "She keeps the pills now."

I feel a dead weight in my stomach, like I'm standing at the edge of the world while the rest of it is crumbling behind me, like soon all that's left will be me on a tiny piece of dirt, surrounded by space.

"Sorry," he says.

All I can do is nod and start walking. I am floating away, around the side of the school and into the rain. I feel the cold drops hit my neck, the wet grass brush against my ankles. That is all I feel. I have skin and nothing else. I am a shell with nothing inside it.

I walk to the pay phone in the front of the school. I call my mom collect.

"Hello?" she says. I can hear the theme music of her favorite video game in the background.

"Mom, can you come pick me up?"

"What's wrong?"

"I'm still sick."

"Sure, okay," she says. "Can you wait an hour? I'm kind of busy right now."

"No," I say. "Come get me now." My voice breaks at the end, whiny, like a child on the verge of a tantrum.

"Okay, okay," she says, not even trying to hide the fact that she'd rather play video games than pick up her daughter, who could be dying.

Our apartment is three miles from school. She will be here any minute. I just need to wait. I can do this. I can wait.

I hear the front door slam against the side of the building. I hear the hard voices of the gangster girls. I see them and their matching red puffy coats. I try hiding behind a pole but it is not thick enough to cover all of me. If I stand still enough, they won't see me. If I don't make a sound, they will never know I am here.

I can see them from where I am hiding. The big one with the face covered in pimples pulls out a cigarette and the little one with the harelip lights it for her. The fat one scratches her crotch.

I stay as still as I can, waiting for the moment my mom's car drives up so I can run to the sidewalk and jump in. I watch the street for her but she's not there. I look back at the gangster girls and they are all looking at me. I moved my head too fast. They see me. They are coming. All three of them are walking toward me and there's nowhere I can go.

"Hey, bitch," the big one says. They are getting closer. I start backing away.

"Hey, princess," the fat one says. "We just want to talk to you." I back into the side of the building, into the sharp edge of the sign that says *Kirkland Junior High*. I rub my bruised hip. There is nowhere to go.

"We heard you been talking shit," says the little one. I shake my head.

"Why you lying?" says the fat one.

"I'm not," I say, my voice high and whiny.

"Why you say all that shit?" says the big one.

"I didn't," I say, trying to back up further, trying to make the wall absorb me. "I didn't say anything."

"You calling me a liar?" says the big one. Her face is in my face. Her breath is cigarettes and fried food.

"No, of course not," I stutter. She is not convinced. She is twice as big as I am. She is so close our noses are practically touching.

I see Mom's car out of the corner of my eye. I breathe.

"My mom's here," I say.

"I don't give a shit," she says.

"I have to go," I say. I step sideways. I find a way out of the trap between her body and the wall. I start walking. I can hear them close behind me. I see Mom looking at us, confused, wondering who my new friends are. I walk faster. They are still behind me. I am touching the door handle. I am lifting it up. I pull but there is nothing. The door is locked. The big girl's hands are on my shoulders. Her voice is in my ears, "Turn around, bitch." My eyes scream, *Unlock the door.* Mom fumbles for the button and I am not breathing and my heart is in my throat. I hear the click of the door unlocking and I squeeze my hand but it is not on the door. It is being pulled away. There is a giant girl behind me turning me around.

There are hands on my shoulders. There is hot breath on my face, reeking of rot. There are hands around my neck. My feet are not on the ground. I feel my back slide up the side of the car. I feel my weight hanging from two fat thumbs lodged in my throat, my eyes popping out of my head, my feet kicking air, my feet kicking the car. I hear the dull thuds on dent-resistant metal. I hear the silence from inside.

This is not happening. I am not here. I am not thinking about my mother as I can't even gasp for air. I'm not thinking about my mother or the hands wrapped around my throat and the pain that runs from my jaw through my spine, my teeth gritting, smashed together, my tongue caged and thrashing, my feet thrashing against air, against dent-resistant metal, my hands clutching at smooth metal that has no holds, my hands gripping at the girl with the man-sized hands, the wrists the size of ankles. I'm not thinking about my mother in the car behind my back. I'm not thinking about the dull, deep thuds she must hear, that she is trying not to hear, even though she's only an arm's reach away, behind glass that does not break no matter how hard I slam against it.

I am on the ground. I cannot see. I hear the girls walking away. I breathe and it feels like bricks inside my chest. I open the door. It is not locked. I put my backpack at my feet. I look straight ahead. The car moves. Mom lights a cigarette with the tip of her old one. Her hands are shaking. She's breathing hard. Smoke stabs my lungs. She looks straight ahead. I cough so hard I want to throw up. She turns on talk radio. Loud.

(TWENTY)

Silence like waves, undulating like nausea. Like methodical punches in the stomach, shoves, rolling earthquake. Silence in the way Mom grips the steering wheel, the way the radio voices blur into the buzz of frequencies, invisible mouths moving, nothing coming out. Shallow breaths release and are chased back in. My throat pulses.

"Mom," I say.

Her hands on the steering wheel, her lips nailed shut.

"Mom," I say, louder.

Her eyes squeezing shut. The car going faster.

"Mom!" I scream. The radio voices scream. My hands grab dashboard as the car brakes just inches before crashing into the truck in front of us. Horns honk from behind. The car settles into its abrupt stillness.

"We have to go to Sarah's house," I say.

Mom doesn't move.

"We have to go now."

She shakes her head slowly.

"Mom, we have to get her."

Nothing.

"Please," I say.

A single tear drops down her cheek. I watch its gentle journey down, watch it settle, suspended at the bottom of her soft chin.

"Turn here," I say.

She does.

"Turn right here," then, "Left here," then, "Stop."

"I'll be right back," I say. She nods, still not looking at me. The tear hanging from her chin has grown. Her cheeks are lined with long, glistening streaks.

I get out of the car. I close the door. I count my steps as I walk to the house. I ring the doorbell. I knock. I wait and hear birds chirping. I knock again. Nothing. I put my hand on the cold doorknob. It turns. The door opens. I smell the familiar stench.

"Sarah," I call into the house. Nothing.

"Sarah!" I yell again. I close the door behind me and it is suddenly, eerily quiet, like this cluttered room is now all that exists, like closing the door destroyed everything that makes sound, all cars, all birds, all lawn mowers and airplanes and voices. It is just me and the house and the absence of Sarah.

"Sarah." My voice is swallowed up by the stained carpet, the walls yellow with smoke, the cobwebby corners, the stacks and piles of garbage and broken things.

I hear slow, wet breaths. I see Lenora on the couch with her eyes closed, in nothing but her underwear and an open bathrobe.

"Hey," I say. She grunts and her body shudders. I navigate across the cluttered floor. I shake her clammy shoulder. I smell the poison seeping out of her pores.

"Lenora!" I yell in her face, and her eyes shoot open and she sits up straight.

"What? What?" she says, looking frantically around the room, finally finding me in front of her.

"Jesus, girl," she says, and lies back down, her eyes heavy again.

"Where's Sarah?" I say.

She's nodding off. Her eyes are closing. I grab both of her shoulders and shake her back awake.

"Where's Sarah, Lenora?"

She looks at me, but her eyes don't focus.

"Gone," she says.

"Gone where?"

"They took her."

"Who took her? The social workers?"

She shakes her head weakly. Her eyes close again.

"Her dad?" I say. "Did her dad take her?" *Oh, God,* I am thinking. *Please God, no.*

Lenora shakes her head. "He didn't get a chance," she slurs. "She's the smart one. Sarah."

"Where is she?" I am losing my patience. I want to slap this woman. I want to hit her hard.

Lenora opens her eyes, and for a moment she seems sober. She looks into my eyes and says with a completely blank face, "She's dead, girl. She took all the pills in the house."

There is a numbness that's greater than all the others, one that is different than floating to the ceiling, different than a wall of fog or an empty shell or stoned stupor or blank space or sheer will. It is numbness that starts with the sharpest pain you've ever felt. There is a dull knife that cuts your heart out. There are giant fists that smash it into a bloody pulp. But then you are left with a cavity, an empty, aching space that can feel nothing but loss, a word, *loss,* abstract and unspecific.

And this is the greatest movie so far. The shot is perfectly composed. The lighting is sinister. The props are all expertly placed: the piles of trash, the cigarette butts, the liquor bottles, the empty fridge. The only sounds are Lenora's wheezing breaths and the dripping faucet in the kitchen. Then the voice-over: "She's dead, girl," again and again until you have to believe it, until the credits roll and the lights come back and you can leave the theater and return to your safe, normal life, untouched by anything, where you can shake off the dying residue of feelings that have nothing to do with you.

She's dead, girl.

She's dead.

"I told them I didn't want her," Lenora says, and her voice sounds far away, fluttering and drab like moth wings. "So they took her. What do you think they're going to do with her?"

Her fingers brush my arm. My skin feels like it's across the room. I see her touch me, but it is seconds before I feel it.

"Hey you," she says, slapping my hand weakly. "I asked you a question."

"I don't know," I say. I am staring at the sweating window, at the smears of color contained in the tiny droplets of water. "I don't know what they do with the bodies."

Bodies. A body. Not Sarah. Just another girl's body that is not useful anymore.

"The bodies," says Lenora as I walk slowly to the door. I can see my legs moving, but I do not feel them.

"Cassie," she says. "Is that your name?"

I keep walking.

"Cassie. Cassandra. What an ugly name."

The birds are still chirping as I walk to the car. My legs are weak, like I have been walking for days. It is not them carrying me. They move out of habit, because they don't know what else to do. I am floating. The birds are somewhere close, but I do not see them.

I open the car door. I get inside. I buckle my seat belt. Mom stares at me. Her face is drenched with fear and love.

I start screaming.

(TWENTY-ONE)

The other day, I found one of your hairs on my blanket. I could tell it was not a hair you pulled out, not part of a clump you tore out of your scalp. It was a single hair, one that fell out naturally, one you never knew was missing. I held it in my fingers and thought it strange that it could exist without your body, that it was the last piece of you anyone would ever see.

Sarah, I put the hair in my mouth. I don't know why, but I pushed it in until it curled on my tongue. I drank stale water from the cup by my bed and felt it slither halfway down my throat. It's a strange feeling to have a hair stuck in your throat, half-tickling, half-choking, like it's trying to climb its way back out, like it's trying to reach sky and air and light.

I drank more water until I couldn't feel it anymore. It was somewhere inside me, but now it's gone. Disintegrated. Turned into nothing.

I wake up these days suspicious, wondering why I slept so well. Then I remember the pills Mom gave me to make me calm down. Then I remember the car ride home. Lenora. Alex. The screaming. You.

And that's when it hits me, the punch in the stomach, the carving out of my insides. That's when I realize that none of this is a movie. I will not go out with a bang. There is no ending. There are no credits. I will wake up and I will keep waking up and this will always be waiting for me.

Or maybe not. Maybe this is the movie where Cassie wakes up to the sound of walkie-talkies and hard knocks at her door. The mother's voice filtered through sleep-fog, "Honey, please wake up." A montage of memories: crowded hallways and big girls, the feeling of choking, the sound of birds chirping, the smell of damp cigarette smoke and rotting food.

You, pale and lifeless. You, with your stomach full of poison. You, sitting on your mattress with a packed suitcase next to you, waiting for someone who never came.

"Cassandra." The girl hears her name. She is not as beautiful as she was at the beginning of the movie. She gets out of bed and opens the door. There are a man and a woman in blue uniforms. All she can see are the guns on their belts. All she can see is the man staring at her nipples through her thin pajama shirt as he says, "We just have some questions to ask you, dear." He sounds kind even as he looks her up and down.

This is the kind of movie where the cops take notes in their little notepads. The mother tells them about the phone calls the girl missed while she was sleeping, death threats from the former best friend. Then it is the girl's turn to explain how it all came to this. This is when everything comes out. This is the purging, the moment of truth, when all secrets become not-secrets, when the cops take notes and make them official. This is the movie with the weeping mother, with the father bursting through the front door at just the right moment, the father who never before left work early, just when the man cop is saying, "We know that family well. We'll make sure she never bothers you again," just when the lady cop is patting the girl's knee, cooing, "It's not your fault." Then the girl cries, falling to the floor in gratitude at this excellent timing, at this synchronized concern, at all of these ears listening. The end.

Or maybe the girl feels nothing. Maybe she is doing what she must to make the phone stop ringing, doing what she must to make the cops go away, to get her house back to normal, to make everything silent like it should be. This could be the movie where nothing changes, where everyone ends up exactly where they started.

Another moving van. Another new school. New girls and new boys who still want the same things.

The daughter on a couch in a small, sterile office, staring at a therapist's leg hair stubble sticking through nylons, staring at the clock on the wall. The sound of *tick, tick, tick*. The walk back to the car, the mother's hopeful face.

"What did you talk about?" the mother asks.

"Nothing," says the girl.

Tick, tick, tick.

A doctor and a prescription pad lined with scribbles. A bottle of pills glittering with hope. The girl puts one in her mouth, swallowing. The pill settles into her stomach. The girl waits for hours for it to kick in, "to take the edge off" like the doctor said, to make everything go away.

But you are still there.

And then it is winter again. The edges of the lake have frozen over, all the life below hidden, suspended. And there is the girl, Cassie, on the shore, just breathing.

Or what if this is a different kind of movie? What if this is a kind of movie that hasn't even been made yet? What if this is my movie, really mine? What if I am the one with the camera in my hand, my fingers on the buttons? What if it is my voice saying stop, go, action, cut? What if I am the one giving all the directions? And I am the actor. And you are the actress. And this is our set, our soundstage, this place that doesn't exist yet, a floating island out in the middle of the ocean, warm water lapping against the sandy shore. This is a place where it is never winter, where there is food everywhere, hanging from trees, waiting for us to eat it, perfectly ripe. We shower in waterfalls. We watch the birds do somersaults in the air, the most beautiful birds you've ever seen, with wings as long as we are tall, red, yellow, orange, feathers like flame. The feathers fall to the ground for us to put in our hair, for us to weave together to make our clothes. There are lakes so clear we can see the bottom lined with diamonds.

There are no shadows, no caves, no dark places where things can hide. There is only you and me and the birds with flame feathers, only soft sand and warm sun and moss for us to sleep on. We will lie on the beach and write songs on each other's skin. We will sing them to the birds and they will sing back. When the sun sets, it will be a different kind of dark. Not dark like suffocation, not like everything gone. Not a dark that can be used against us. It will simply be dark like sleeping, dark like heavy eyes.

We will build a fire with feathers. We will watch the light dance on each other's faces. It will keep us warm but it will not burn us. Because it's fire that is ours, fire that we made. Can you feel it? Hold your hands out and wave them a little. Look, you can wave the smoke in any direction, into any shape. These are our smoke signals, puffs of white in the night air only we can read. We will build a fire bigger than any fire that's ever existed. The smoke will be strong enough to cross an ocean. Maybe one of our smoke rings, one of our Morse code letters, will travel somewhere we haven't been yet. It will reach land and someone will see it and they will wonder what it means.

But for now, there is no island. You are gone and this is not a movie. For now, there is only a new school in a new city, new teachers and new students who never knew who I was before. There is me with a naked face and my hair in a ponytail, trying not to be seen. There is a scholarship with my name on it and an expensive classroom with desks arranged in a circle. There are students who speak without raising their hands. A teacher who listens. Nodding and thoughtful hands on chins. There are strangers looking at the new girl. They are looking at me and wanting me to speak.

I am sitting at my desk, listening to everyone talk about Dostoyevsky. I am trying not to look up, trying not to show how much I want to be in on this conversation, trying not to show how much I want to say. I am holding my pencil too tight. I put it down so I won't break it. I stare at my blank notebook, trying to make the blue lines move.

And then there is something in front of me, a foreign object covered with lines and squiggles that are not mine. I look up and the girl next to me smiles, her freckles so perfect she could be Annie. I squint and look closer. I scour the white skin, the red curls, the blue eyes for cruelty. But all she's doing is smiling. All she did was put her notebook on my desk, turned to a page with a picture I do not recognize.

It is a drawing, a penciled comic. It is a room full of ducks arranged in a circle, their cartoon beaks open, the dialogue bubbles spelling *Quack!* At the bottom of the page, at one edge of the circle, sit two geese, one with a ponytail, the other with curly hair and freckles. The freckled goose says, "Hi, I'm Chelsea."

I pick up my pencil and write words for the other.

Cassandra. Nice to meet you.

ACKNOWLEDGMENTS

Thank you
Thank you
Thank you

To my parents, who always supported my creativity and weirdness, even when it was loud and messy. You knew, even when I didn't, that all those messes were just part of the plan.

To my mentors and teachers and readers: Lisa Rosenberg, Sarah Stone, Edie Meidav, Brian Teare, Daphne Gottlieb, Felicia Ward, Carolyn Cooke, Helen Klonaris, Chris Savino, everyone in Writing & Consciousness at New College, and so many more. Your wisdom and support made me a better writer than I'd ever be on my own.

To my agent, Amy Tipton, who believed in me when I was starting not to—with that first phone call, you gave me a taste of what it feels like to have a dream come true. And to Anica Rissi at Simon Pulse—I am truly blessed to have an editor who gets my work as well as you do.

And finally—to my fantastic, amazing, adorable, and talented husband Brian. This never would have happened without you. Your love makes me brave.